CHRISTMAS WITH MARY BROWN

BERNICE BLOOM

Bernice Bloom

HELLO LOVELY READERS

Thank you so much for joining Mary Brown for Christmas.

This is the fourth book in the series, but it can easily be read as a stand-alone book.

Christmas is a wonderful time for our rather bonkers heroine because she ADORES it and embraces the build-up to the big day with all the delight and joy of a toddler seeing jelly babies.

This little book features Mary's role as the chief decorator of the Beckhams' Christmas tree, lots of ginger wine, and a wild confession to Holly Willoughby. Then there's the trip to Lapland, a date to remember & two Christmas lunches.

I hope you enjoy it.

Lots of love,

Bernie x

THE ORDER OF THE MARY BROWN BOOKS

IMPORTANT NOTE:

This book was previously released as 'Adorable Fat Girl at Christmas.'

FOSTERS DIY STORE

1

3th December: 12 days til Christmas

'Mary Brown, Mary Brown. Please go to the store manager's office. The store manager's office, immediately.'

Oh, bloody hell, this isn't going to be good. I put down the spades I am arranging in height order in the gardening section (I'm just trying to look busy - there's no reason on God's earth why the spades should be assembled in height order). I walk out of the enormous conservatory, pass the rows of plants and trundle into the main store, heading to the manager's office.

I'm wearing my bright green overalls and a red hat and gloves. I don't think anyone has ever looked less attractive (I resemble a large, wobbly poinsettia). It's just so cold over in the gardening section; any thoughts about appearance have been washed away by a wave of desire to stay warm.

I'm working in the gardening section this week because I want to be around all the Christmas trees. I thought it would be all festive and fun. But, tragically, it's not. They haven't got one tree that's nicely decorated. Not one! And there's no music, lights, or any of the lovely Christmassy things you need to make the place look great.

This state of affairs brings me considerable distress because I love Christmas; I adore it. If I were running this place, all the staff would be dressed like Santa, giving out presents to kids, singing carols and being jolly and friendly. Others I've spoken to disagree. They say that most people want to come into a DIY shop, buy a hammer and go home - not be confronted by a bunch of idiots singing 'We wish you a Merry Christmas' in homemade tinsel hats.

'OOHH, SOMEONE'S IN TROUBLE,' says Neil as I pass the shelving aisle where he appears to be arranging pieces of wood in size order.

He's heard the announcement calling me to the manager's office and assumes I've done something wrong.

'No, Keith wants to talk to me about a pay rise,' I say.

'Yeah, right. Because Keith is *always* doing that.'

I give him a smile and a shrug of my shoulders, but Neil's probably right. I am bound to be in trouble. Why else would I be summoned over the public address system? It'll be because of my joke yesterday: a guy was buying a screwdriver in the hardware section, and I was working on the tills. He came over to pay, and at the same time, as I put the digits into the card machine, his phone rang. It made me laugh because it was as if I'd just dialled him, so I picked up the card reader and pretended it was a phone...holding it to my ear and saying, 'Hello, anyone there.' In my head, it was hysterical, and to the guy's credit, he did laugh weakly at me when I did it.

But the trouble started when I brushed the machine against my ear, and I managed to add extra zeros to the total, so the screwdriver ended up costing £1900. It was quite a fiasco when the guy's bank rejected the payment. Then we realised what I'd done. He wasn't laughing so much then.

I'm pretty sure that'll be what Keith wants to discuss with me - my wholly unprofessional behaviour.

I walk into Keith's office and decide to front up straight away in the hope that this will minimise the anger he feels towards me.

'Sorry about pretending the card machine was a phone,' I say. 'It won't happen again.'

'The card machine? What are you talking about?'

Oh good. It's not that. That's a relief. It must be the other thing I did yesterday.

'If it's not the card machine that you want to talk to me about, then I'd like to say I'm sorry about the lipstick kisses,' I say. 'I know that was unprofessional, but the customers didn't object. No one complained. It was a bit of light-hearted fun.'

'What lipstick kisses?' he asks.

Oh no.

'Um. Well, I was working on the paint mixing counter, and when people place an order, we give them a receipt and tell them to come back in an hour to collect the paint.'

'Yes, I know you do, Mary. I implemented that system.'

'Well, I put *'see you in an hour'* and a lipstick kiss - it was just a bit of fun...I thought that's what you wanted to see me about.'

'Er...no,' says Keith, with a bemused look on his red face.'I'm calling you in because I want you to be in charge of Christmas.'

'In charge of Christmas? What do you mean?'

It sounds like the best job in the world, ever.

'You know - make the store look Christmassy, organise some Christmas events. The place is looking a bit unloved. Could you make it look festive?'

'Oh God, yes,' I say, rising to my feet and just about resisting the urge to throw my arms around his thick, florid neck and kiss his bald patch. 'I've never been up for anything more in my entire life.'

'Good,' he says. 'Have a ponder and come back to me with a list of what you think we should be doing. You have a budget of £250.'

'OK,' I say, beaming.

'Oh, and Mary…'

'Yes.'

'Stop doing that lipstick kiss thing.'

'Of course,' I say. 'I won't do it again.'

I walk out of Keith's office and do a little jig. Not a full-on dance or anything - I'm British, after all - just a little shuffle to reflect the happiness inside me. Then I smile. I'm in charge of bloody Christmas.

BATTLE OF THE PARENTS

*W*hen I get home from work, the phone rings in my flat. I always answer the landline with extreme caution because it's usually someone trying to sell me something or convince me that I've been in an accident that wasn't my fault. There have been times when the woman on the phone has been so convincing that I have come away believing I was in an accident. Maybe someone knocked into my car, and I wasn't at fault? It could have happened. Then I remember that I can't drive and don't have a car.

'Hello Mary, it's mum.'

Yes - that's the other thing I should have mentioned about the landline: if it's not a salesman, it's mum. Everyone else in the world now rings me on my mobile, but not my mother.

'I'm in charge of Christmas!' I blurt out. There's a moment's silence.

'Very good,' she says before moving on. 'As a special treat, we thought it would be nice to invite Ted to come to us for Christmas. Do you think he'd like to?'

I have to tell you - this is a most unusual development. My Dad is not fond of visitors. So for mum to invite anyone round, knowing what dad's like, is a miracle, and for them to ask a boyfriend of mine...someone they haven't even met yet...well, that's plain madness.

'I think he'd love to,' I say, feeling a shiver of excitement at the thought of waking up on Christmas morning in my flat with Ted and then walking hand-in-hand with him to mum and dad's house.

'Good,' says mum. 'Then I'll ensure we have enough food for all of us. I told your father I was inviting Ted, and he said he was looking forward to meeting him.'

I know this isn't true. Dad hates meeting anyone new.

'Oh, and we're getting a new freezer. Did I tell you?'

Again, this is surprising news. For most people, a new freezer might not be a huge deal, but for mum and dad - it's more significant news than if she told me that dad was getting a sex change. They don't ever buy anything new. They are all about 'make do and mend' - it's like the Blitz is going on, and they feel duty-bound not to use up the country's precious, dwindling resources.

'We've talked about it for a few years and decided to get one before Christmas. Will you help me choose one?'

'Of course, I will,' I say.

'Very good. Talk to you soon.'

Whenever I speak to mum on the phone, I'm astonished by how clipped her tones are and how formal and professional she sounds; it's as if she's talking on the telephone for the first time. As if phones have just been invented, and she's not at all sure whether they're a good idea. She's not at all like that in real life. Still - nice of her to invite Ted to Christmas. I'm chuffed about that.

LATER THAT EVENING, I arrive at Ted's flat, eager to give him the double helping of good news that I have been put in charge of Christmas and that he has been invited to spend Christmas Day with my parents and me. I'm not sure how he'll react to the latter of these two pieces of information because he's never met my parents. But now that Ted and I have been going out together for six months, it's time he met them, and Christmas will be the perfect opportunity.

He opens the door beaming with delight. It's like he knows my good news.

'You look happy,' I say.

'I'm delighted, young lady,' he says, pulling me into his arms. 'Come in, and I'll tell you all about it.'

Ted closes the door behind me, and I start walking up the narrow staircase to his flat. I hate walking ahead of Ted. I'm always worried that he's looking at my colossal bottom and wondering whether he'd be better off with someone who wasn't the size of a large freight ship. I worry that he'll go off me or something. Not that he's thin. We met at Fat Club and are both...how do I phrase this elegantly?...we're both considerably larger than Kate Moss. We've lost some weight and are on mad diets most of the time, but we still both weigh twice what an average person does.

We get to the top (only about ten steps), and I'm breathing heavily...I need to start exercising as well as dieting.

'I'm in charge of Christmas!' I blurt out.

'OK, you'll never guess where we've been invited,' he says.

Why is no one reacting in how I expect them to act to the news that I am IN CHARGE OF CHRISTMAS? Surely that statement deserves some recognition, but first, mum completely ignored me, and now Ted has completely ignored me.

'I'm in charge of Christmas,' I repeat.

'I know. You said. Well done, you. Now - you have to guess where we've been invited to go.'

No one is anywhere near as excited by my news as I am.

'Buckingham Palace?' I venture.

'Better.'

'Better than Buckingham Palace? Um...The White House? Is that better? I don't know. Tell me.'

'OK. Wait for this...my mum and dad have invited us to have Christmas lunch with them. I can't believe it. It's so exciting. My sister's away for Christmas, and they thought we might like to join them instead. Please, please, please say 'yes'.'

'Um... yes,' I say before I can stop myself and explain that I have already committed to lunch with my parents after they made an extraordinary invitation. But I don't want to let Ted down; he looks so excited. And it is wonderful that his parents have invited me to join them for Christmas. I'm flattered. Perhaps I can pull out later...urge him to change his mind and come with me to my parents instead.

'Brilliant,' he says, gathering me up and kissing me all over my face. 'You've made me the happiest man alive. Now I can't wait for Christmas day. It's going to be the best.'

Shit.

We retire to bed with glasses of wine. Ted is beaming with happiness that we will be spending Christmas at his mum's; I am smiling and trying to look like it's a great idea.

'What did you say earlier?' he asks. 'Something about you wanting to take charge of Christmas.'

'No, I've taken charge of Christmas. I am now in charge. It's official.'

'I think you'll find Father Christmas already has that job sewn up, sweetheart. What are you talking about?'

'I'm talking about work...Keith called me into his office today and told me he wants me to be in charge of Christmas.'

'Wow, that's brilliant,' says Ted.

Finally, someone recognises what a big deal this is.

'You'll be perfect.'

'Yes - I know. I'm beyond excited about it,' I say. 'I have many plans to decorate the store and offer a Christmas tree decorating service and lollipops for children. I have to pitch all my ideas to Ted in the morning.'

'Well done you,' says Ted, kissing me lightly on the cheek before rolling over and going to sleep. I drift off, too, thinking of how to make Fosters DIY Emporium the best Christmas experience ever.

We need a nativity scene...a brilliant one. We should have real donkeys. Where can you get real donkeys? And we need a baby Jesus. Can you hire them? I need to check that. We need a giant Christmas tree with beautiful lights, presents underneath it, and a star on top, and we need lots of Father Christmases and carols playing and sweets for children and the smell of mulled wine and mince pies, and maybe Christmas cards for every customer.

And why don't we have a magical Post Box where people can post their Christmas wishes? Then someone could answer all the letters. I'll make this the best Christmas ever for everyone who comes into the store.

BEING MARY CHRISTMAS

1 4th December

At 9 am the following morning, I am standing in front of Keith with my list of ideas typed out neatly on a sheet of A4.

'I thought we could have a Christmas postbox of wishes and dreams, a nativity scene, lots of decorations and lots of fun,' I say as he scans the list, nodding to himself. What he's worried about, of course, is the cost. He reminds me that he told me to keep to a £250 budget.

'Yeah, the budget is a bit tight, but I thought we could get the local paper to come down,' I say. 'Editors like Christmas pictures in the paper, so if we had an amazing nativity scene, they might photograph it, then we'd be in the papers, and we'd attract more customers. Then your boss would be thrilled.'

You see: I may look stupid in my large green overall and with Christmas decorations hanging from my ears (are they too much?), but I'm not. I know that the prospect of free publicity will be enough to compel him to spend a fortune.

'Indeed,' says Keith, with a sharp rise of his eyebrows.

'Excellent thinking. And then, we can offset the costs against the PR budget. Perfect. Get to it, Mary. Christmas is in six days, so we need to get cracking.

Tomorrow is the day when celebrations officially start at the centre, so use today to get everything set up.

'Great,' I say, adjusting the tinsel in my hair. 'The only thing is - I'm supposed to be working on the till in the bathroom section this afternoon. It will take a while to do all this. Could someone else cover, so I can sit down and sort this out?'

'Yes, of course,' says Keith, hitting the microphone and buzzer on his desk. 'Could the supervisor in the bathrooms section please come to the manager's office immediately? Thank you,' he says.

'Mary, go and work on the desk next to Sharon. Let's try and get this place Christmas-ed up to the hilt by the end of the day, and I want photographers and BBC news film crews here tomorrow.'

'Right,' I say. Keith seems to have escalated the publicity potential in his mind. The 10 O'clock news has replaced my suggestion of a local newspaper. How do you convince a TV crew to come to a DIY store?

I'd have thought they would have better things to do.

Presumably, they wouldn't come unless a child was kidnapped or something.

Maybe I should kidnap a... But, no, I can't do that.

I sit next to perfect Sharon in her elegant cream suit (not for her the daily humiliation of a green overall), and I start scribbling.

The first thing I have to do is create a very realistic nativity scene. I'll need a baby, a Mary and Jesus, wise men, shepherds and some animals. That can't be too hard to assemble, can it? The average junior school production manages to acquire all of those, so it can't be beyond me.

'It's nice to have a girl working alongside me,' says Sharon, smiling at me warmly.

'Yes,' I say, but I don't want to engage in chit-chat; I want to organise a wonderful Christmas. So I lean over my notebook and scribble away.

Sharon watches me.

'Mary, you might be able to help me with this,' she says. 'Something's been troubling me.'

'Has it?'

'Yes, I saw on the telly last night that they said one in three men lives at home now.'

'OK,' I say. 'That doesn't surprise me. It's a sign of the times...credit crunch and all that. People are finding it difficult to buy their own homes.'

'No, but it's ridiculous...everyone lives at home.'

'Yes, but they mean that one in three men lives in the family home rather than buying their own home.'

'But it's still a home.'

'Yes, but they mean they don't have their own homes.'

'But they do have homes.'

Oh goodness.

'You're right,' I say, eager to return to my Christmas planning. 'How silly of them.'

'Isn't she adorable?' says Keith, standing over Sharon as we chat. 'Mary, I'm fortunate to have someone as smart and lovely as my PA.'

'You are,' I say, looking up at him as he grins down at her, and she turns scarlet in response. Keith does have more than a touch of the David Brents. Everything he does is ever-so-slightly cringey.

'Come on, Sharon, let me take you to lunch as a Christmas treat. Then, Mary, maybe you could cover the office while we're out?'

'Sure,' I reply, as Sharon pulls her brush from her handbag

and starts sprucing herself up for lunch with the boss. It's striking the difference it makes to your life if you're pretty, delicate and alluring like Sharon. I see the guys rushing to open doors for her and help her if she has anything heavy to carry. Me? Nope - I'm left to struggle with my arms full - bashing doors open with my enormous arse while men stand by, ogling at women like Sharon.

'See you later,' she squeaks, wiggling her way out of the office and leaving me to my planning.

Their lunch seems like a triumph because they don't reappear that afternoon. So I sit there, lost in my own world, plotting and planning until around 7 pm when I pack up everything and head home.

On the way home that evening, I jump off the bus at a toy store to collect everything I need for my nativity scene, along with decorations for the garden centre. They come to £275. I've smashed through the budget after a little shopping trip. Still, it had to be done. Keith says that Christmas officially starts tomorrow, so I must be prepared. When I get home, I line up all the animals in the hallway and look at them like a proud mother—what a splendid selection. I'm thrilled that I've got this job…bloody thrilled.

TEN DAY COUNT-DOWN BEGINS

1 5th December

The following day, I'm awake at the crack of dawn. 'It's Christmaaaaaaas....' I yell into Ted's ear in the manner of Nodder Holder. He jumps as he wakes up and throws his big hands against his ears, muttering obscenities at me. Then he pulls the duvet over his head and turns away. So my words of seasonal joy haven't had quite the effect on my beloved that I hoped they might.

Most people would take this as a sign that their partner doesn't want to be disturbed and walk away. Not me. I'm not perturbed. Nothing can dampen the Christmas spirit soaring through my veins. So I sit up and start singing *Twelve Days of Christmas*.

'On what planet is it Christmas today?' Ted shouts over the sound of my awful singing. 'It's 15th December. That's not Christmas Day anywhere.'

'No, not Christmas Day,' I say. 'It's Christmas time. Today the countdown to Christmas starts at work. And you remember who's in charge of it all, don't you?'

There's a long sigh and a grumpy noise from the lump under the duvet.

'Meeeeeeee,' I remind him.

Ted sits up and rubs his eyes.

'I can build my lovely nativity scene today and put up the magic *Post Box of Wishes and Dreams*. Also, we'll start giving sweets to all the children who come to the store, which will be lovely.'

'Yeah, I'd be a bit cautious about handing sweets to children. That can end badly.'

'Nonsense,' I tell him as I get changed for work. This morning I don't have to clamber into the terrible green uniform that makes me look like a cross between Kermit and Shrek. No, I'm not working on the tills for the next 12 days, so I put on my red Christmas jumper with big holly leaves on the front. The great joy of this jumper is that, in addition to the fact that it has big holly leaves on the front, it also has Christmas baubles all over the back, and when you press each of the baubles, it plays a different festive tune.

Of course, Ted looks at me like I'm nuts and comments that I constantly moan about having to wear the horrible green uniform to work. He says I complain about not being able to wear nice clothes, then as soon as I get the opportunity to wear my own stuff, I opt for a ridiculous Christmas jumper.

'But this is nice,' I say. 'I like it. It's fun, musical and charming. Now, I need to go. Don't delay me any longer.'

'Don't delay you? I was fast asleep. You woke me up.'

'Oh yes - sorry about that. Right, I'm going. See you later.'

I go to the kitchen and collect a large bin bag to transport all the stuffed animals waiting patiently by the front door.'

Ted follows me, rubbing his eyes like a giant toddler.

'Are these the animals for the nativity scene?' he says, as he watches me laying them carefully into a bin bag.

'Yes.'

'But they're ridiculous.'

'What's wrong with them? They'll make the nativity scene look wonderful.'

'An elephant, a camel and a horse? In the name of all that is holy, where do they fit in? There wasn't an elephant in the stable.'

'That's how the three wise men got to Bethlehem.'

'Yeah, on an elephant? Sure.'

'It's true. One was on an elephant, one on a camel, and the other on a horse. I know I'm right because I phoned the vicar from the toy shop last night to be sure.'

'Was the vicar sober?'

I stand there, looking down at the bin bag, not keen to discuss this anymore because I want to be excited about it and have a lovely time.

'Why are you in a sulk?' asks Ted.

'I'm not in a sulk, I just know how the three wise men got to Bethlehem, and you don't, so keep your nose out of my elephant-related business.'

'OK,' he says, unsure whether I'm serious or joking.

I run out to the bus with my bag of animals and catch it in the nick of time. I sit down but soon realise I have to perch on the edge because every time I move back, my jumper touches the seat and bursts into song. I didn't realise it was quite so sensitive. One little knock and my jumper starts serenading me. I see people looking at their phones, wondering whether an incoming text is causing the sudden musical outburst.

I'm about halfway through the journey when I burst into song without touching my jumper. It takes me a few minutes to realise that it's my phone, with a text from Ted.

'Can you get me some deodorant if you pass a shop? I'm

stuck in the office all day, and I'm starting to smell like a horse, a camel and an elephant! Xxx'

Given the unhelpful jibe about my nativity animals, he doesn't deserve any, but since I get off the bus next to Boots, I'll get some for him.

It's one of those tiny branches of Boots that sells nothing but the absolute essentials. I walk in and head to where the deodorants are kept, but there only appear to be women's deodorants. Do you think it matters? I mean - what difference can it make? It must be all the same inside, just with different patterns.

But I know Ted won't be happy if I come back with a pink, floral deodorant bottle, so I ask the somewhat official-looking woman behind the counter, wearing a white uniform, whether she has any men's deodorant.

'The ball kind?' she says.

Ball kind?

'No,' I screech. 'My boyfriend wants it for his underarms, thank you very much.'

Good grief. I didn't even realise you could buy deodorant for your testicles.

When I arrive at Fosters Gardening and DIY centre, I'm still concerned that there are men all over the country rolling deodorant all over their manly bits. But I try to push the unfortunate image out of my mind as I head straight to Keith's office and over to my little desk in the corner, now the centre of all Christmas-related affairs.

It gives me such a sense of importance to have my own desk. I've been working at the centre since I left school. I'm usually out in the store, avoiding customers and their questions and wasting time by moving plants about unnecessarily. But now I have a mission... I'm in charge of something. Christmas is all mine, and I have a desk of my own on which to plan it.

I made a good start yesterday, but I want to discuss things with Keith before proceeding much more. I find him sitting in the cafeteria with horror and sadness etched on his face. He's staring out into the middle distance, contemplative…as if trying to make sense of some terrible event that has befallen him.

'Lord above,' he says when he sees me. 'I drank so much yesterday that I almost killed myself.'

'Oh dear, well, I'm glad you didn't…you know…kill yourself,' I say. 'Have you got five minutes so I can run through some thoughts?'

He looks like he might burst into tears at any moment and slips on his sunglasses.

'Go ahead.'

'I had a good think yesterday while you were out and about, and I made a few calls. This is what we need: first of all - an enormous nativity scene, and I've bought lots of animals with which to fill it. Then we need to decorate eight Christmas trees, have a spectacular light display, and a *Christmas Post Box of Wishes and Dreams* in red and white for people to post their Christmas wishes.

'What I thought we could do is - I could read the letters and answer them from Santa's elf. We know it'll be mainly adults putting notes in there because we don't get that many children in the store. All the same, I think it will be good fun.'

'Sure, whatever,' says Keith. He looks worse now than when I first walked in.

'Is it OK to use Ray and Joe to help me?'

'Why would you do that?'

'I need some help, and in the message you left me last night, you said that they would do the heavy lifting for me.'

'Did I send you a message?'

'You sent lots, but I couldn't establish what you were trying to say in some of them. Shall I show you?'

'No, no. That's fine. Whatever you want. Just go and get on with it.'

'Great,' I say, walking away. I think Keith would have agreed to anything to get rid of me. A perfect scenario. So why the hell didn't I ask for a pay rise?

CHRISTMAS WORLD

I grab a coffee and head out to find Ray and Joe. They are surprised that they are seconded to help me set up Christmas, having not been told anything about the plans by our hung-over boss. But they are pleased to be dragged away from loading fertiliser bags onto the cart at the back of the garden centre.

'First, let's get this nativity scene up and running,' I say, handing each of them a box containing all manner of nativity features, the bag of animals I brought from home, a giant star and some hay.

'I'm afraid we will have to make a new stable. I tried to save the one from last year, but someone had put spider plants on top of it, and it was all dented and horrible, with worms crawling through it. It would have been very disrespectful to expect Mary and Joseph to live in a shabby old stable like that.'

Ray and Joe nod in agreement as I present them with an enormous furniture packing box that I found in the garden furniture department. It is big enough for me to get inside (I know that because I did just that), and I suggest that the guys paint it and move it to my specially chosen location, marked with an 'x' on a map, then fill it with nativity items.

'This area will be henceforth called 'Christmas World'', I say grandly.

'It will contain Santa's grotto and the nativity scene, with Mary and Joseph in the middle, flanked by the three wise men.'

We decide that Ray will work on sorting out the nativity scene while Joe works with me on decorating the trees. I picked up everything I needed for the trees last night and plan to decorate them with my usual verve and individuality by hanging pictures of Rick Astley stuck onto cardboard bells all over one of them.

Rick lives locally, you see, and he has promised to pop in and do a live song for us this Christmas, so it seems appropriate to have one tree decked out with his face. The other trees are slightly soberer, well – I say that, but one has pink elephants hanging from every branch, and the other has a mixture of brightly coloured ornaments. I designed that to be a treat for everyone - a streak of wonder, colour and life.

Lots of the staff gather around as we assemble all the elements of the Christmas scene. As it comes together, it immediately lifts the look of the store (and - to be fair - it's quite a task to lift the appearance of a shop that sells lots of spades and copper piping).

The Christmas World area is now a riot of vibrant hues, sounds and joy. I commandeer a considerable number of lights and the centre's hi-fi system, and we finish this first stage off by playing Christmas music as we string the lights above the whole area, like a sparkly net overhead. The lights move from tree to tree and from the edge of the portacabin to Santa's grotto. You can see the section for miles off. You can probably see it from Mars.

The only thing left to go up is the *Christmas Post Box of*

Wishes and Dreams, which I am lovingly creating from numerous cereal boxes and an old Santa Claus outfit made from horrible scratchy nylon. The result divides opinion. In my view, it's pretty spectacular. In everyone else's view, it's ridiculous.

I put a laminated note in front of the post-box saying:

'Ho, ho, ho. I am the Christmas Post Box of Wishes and Dreams. Post your letters here with all your Christmas wishes, and I will see whether we can make them come true... from Santa's Elf.

'Well, well, well,' says Keith, walking up behind me. 'This looks great.'

'Welcome to Christmas World,' I say. 'Isn't it fabulous?'

'Outstanding, Mary Brown. OOOOh, but I wouldn't put that note on the post box. You'll get all sorts of odd requests.'

'I'm sure I won't,' I say confidently.

'You don't know what guys are like,' he replies as if he were some worldly lothario instead of the inefficient manager of a struggling DIY centre on the outskirts of Cobham.

'You'll be inundated with obscene requests and offensive suggestions,' he adds. 'And that'll be from me. Ha ha. I am only joking. You know I'm joking. Mary. You know I'm joking?'

'Yes, Keith. I know you're joking.'

'Seriously though, I think it's a big mistake to call it a *Christmas Post Box of Wishes and Dreams* – call it a *Christmas Post Box*. You're not going be making anyone's wishes and dreams come true. You are giving them false promises...false hope.'

I try to argue that I am doing no such thing, but Keith's not interested...his attention has wandered, and he's noticed the lattice of lights sparkling above us.

'It's very bright. Very eye-catching. That is a lot of lights.'

'Yes.'

'It lights up the whole nativity scene. Hang on. Why's there an elephant there?'

'That's how one of the three wise men got to Bethlehem.'

'On an elephant? Please do me a favour, Mary. They were on camels; everyone knows that.'

There are sniggers from Ray and Joe.

'One of them came on an elephant. I checked with a vicar.'

My patience is already wearing thin with all the elephant-defending, and I fear this is only the beginning.

'OK. Well, it looks odd. Mary - I've got some of the staff together for a meeting at 4.30 pm. Can you come and give them a quick overview of plans for Christmas and what to expect?'

'Sure,' I say. I don't know what sort of plans Keith thinks I've got. I had a budget of £250, and I've spent about £400 if you include all the pink elephants and pictures of Rick Astley.'

Still, at 4.30 pm, I head to the meeting and walk to the front of the room, preparing to tell all my colleagues about the extraordinary Christmas events we have planned.

'Hello, everyone. As you know, my name is Mary Brown, and I'm in charge of Christmas,' I say proudly. 'I want to run through some of the exciting things we've planned for this year and answer any questions you might have. Also, if you have any questions relating to Christmas or Christmas products, I'll be around to answer all your queries. So, let's get started....'

I run through all the glorious decorations that are now adorning the walls, trees and plants, turning the DIY store into a spectacle of Christmas joy. There's not much reaction, to be honest. I hoped it would be a bit like one of those Trump rallies where cheers and whoops of delight meet everything you say and waving of arms and chanting accompanies every comment, but it doesn't happen like that.

Everyone sits there, mostly looking down, appearing to pay very little attention to what I'm saying. Meanwhile, I bounce around in front of them, full of the joys of the season, squeezing the back of my jumper occasionally to inject some Christmas music and spirit into the occasion and trying to make just one of them smile.

'OK, I'm glad that's all been received so well,' I say. 'Now I want to tell you about an exciting new development this year.

'We will have a *Christmas Post Box of Wishes and Dreams* so that people can put their Christmas wishes into it, and Santa's elf will reply to them all.'

I look around the audience. Tony-the-Tap from bathroom supplies is playing with his phone, and Gavin from outdoor furniture is scratching his ears. I think that might be because he's got nits, though. Gavin's always sporting some horrible health condition, and we mostly keep away from him in case we catch it. Then I see his hand go up.

'Yes, Gavin?'

'How have you got an elf to answer the questions?'

'No, Gavin, it's not a real elf. That was just a joke.'

'Oh, so why are people going to post their Christmas wishes in the box?'

'It's just a bit of Christmas fun. I'll be replying to them.'

'Will you be dressed as an elf?'

'Probably not. It doesn't make any difference. It's just a bit of fun.'

Tony's hand goes up then.

'Do you have to have a stamp on the letter you put in the letterbox?'

'No, Tony. It's not a real letterbox.'

'What will you do if people put stamps on the letters?'

'I haven't thought about that. Perhaps I will take the stamps off the envelopes and give them to charity.'

'What charity?'

'Honestly, I haven't thought about that. I'll ask Keith what he thinks.'

'Do you think that the Mary and Joseph story is true?' asks Martina, the lady who works in the staff canteen.

'I don't know,' I say. 'I'm not a history expert, and I don't have any religious studies background; they've just put me in charge of making the place look Christmassy. I've got some flashing Father Christmas hats here for everyone to wear. I'd be grateful if you could all start wearing them, so we look as festive as possible.'

Another hand goes up. It's Tony-the-Tap again. 'What's with all the elephants in the manger?"

Keith interrupts and says that, unfortunately, we will leave it there, and he hopes everyone enjoys getting into the spirit of Christmas.

CAR SURFING

'*I* need a drink,' I say to Belinda as I slump into an armchair in the coffee room.

'There were some full-on, daft questions being asked there,' she says sympathetically. 'Is it always like this?'

Belinda is new. She's the only woman working in the store around my age; everyone else is much older. I don't think she can believe how slow and behind the times some of them are.

'It's always like this,' I say.

She smiles.

'I think you're amazing. You're a sales assistant like me, but you have taken on all the responsibility for Christmas. I would never be able to stand up and talk in front of everyone like that.'

'Thank you.'

'You should be in charge of this place. You seem so much brighter and more intelligent than everyone else.'

'Gosh, that would be nice. Especially the pay rise,' I say.

'Yeah.' She's playing with the rim of her plastic cup as she sits there in silence. It feels like she wants to ask me something, so I sit there in silence, sipping my coffee.

'Can I ask you a question?' she says eventually. But then Tony-the-Tap walks in, and she looks up, all alarmed. She pulls her chair closer to mine.

'It's quite personal. Can I talk to you away from work? I don't know whether you fancy going for a drink tonight. I'm having a bit of an issue, and I could do with talking it through. A guy is coming on to me, and I'm finding it awkward.'

'Sure,' I say. 'Who is it?'

She glances up at Tony.

'Do you mind if we talk about it later?' she mouths.

'No problem.'

There's a moment's silence.

'Could you give me a clue?'

'No,' says Belinda. 'Let's talk about it tonight. I don't want anyone to overhear. I've got my car; I could drive us.'

'That would be great,' I say. Clearly, I will have to wait until tonight to hear who has been misbehaving. 'Shall I meet you in the car park at 6? My car's a blue Golf.'

'See you then,' I say.

The rest of the day flies past. The staff don't seem to be wildly engaged with my Christmas festivities; some walk around without their flashing Father Christmas hats. To make it worse, they run away whenever they see me approaching, clutching the hats they should be wearing.

Happily, the customers seem to like what they see. First, they come wheeling through the store, then they stop and stare at the festive scene, smiling up at the lights twinkling above them.

People laugh at the Christmas trees and take pictures of my Rick Astley baubles. Then they hover by the nativity scene, humming to the music. There's a genuine feeling of goodwill and delight at the spiderweb of flashing, sparkling lights strung across the top of the nativity section.

By 6 pm, I'm feeling much better about everything. The team meeting put a dampener on things, and the attitude of the staff made me cross but seeing the customers enjoying it has lifted my spirits. I've not seen anyone post a letter in my fabulous postbox yet, but hopefully, by the time I come in tomorrow morning, there'll be a little bundle of them waiting for me.

Now I'm off to meet Belinda for a proper girly natter and also – obviously – to find out which one of our employees has wandering hands.

I've thought about the options since she first mentioned what happened to her. There's Keith - he can be a bit slimy, but I don't think he's the handsy type. The guys in the warehouse are very loud and boisterous when they're all together, but they're pack animals; I can't imagine them causing any trouble when they're on their own without backup.

I walk out to the car park and see Belinda's car straight away...it's all shiny and new-looking, she must have bought it quite recently, or she keeps it looking nice. Funny - she doesn't strike me as the sort of woman who would spend a lot of time looking after her car. She doesn't seem like the sort of woman who spends a lot of time looking after anything. I mean, she's nice but sort of scruffy and poorly put together. I don't mean that as an insult at all; it's just that she's always messy.

As I walk over to her car, I see her coming out of the centre towards us, so I drape myself across the bonnet to await her arrival. I assume an amusing supermodel pose, lying perfectly still, with the poutiest of lips. I lay there for quite a while, thinking that Belinda should be here by now. Perhaps she forgot something and had to rush back inside for it? But, when I look up, she's nowhere to be seen. I'll stay a bit longer but turn onto my other side because this is starting to get uncomfortable. I roll over, feeling the suspension groan beneath me. And then I see it.

Bloody hell.

Sitting in the front of the car, staring at me with a look of wide-eyed confusion, are an elderly man and woman. They look both astonished and terrified. I smile at them to placate them, but judging by how the man flinches and moves back in his seat, he's not remotely reassured.

I scramble off the bonnet, regretting how it dips down as I move across it, and I hope I haven't wrecked their suspension with my antics. Then I wave and run off. I don't know what else to do. I've no idea how to explain to them why I lay across the front of their car for 10 minutes, licking my lips and pouting.

I hear a toot and turn around to see Belinda waving at me while sitting in the driving seat of a scruffy old car. Much more like the sort of vehicle I was expecting her to drive. The thing is practically falling apart. I jump into the passenger seat and instruct her to go.

'Who were they?' she asks, indicating the people sitting in the car on which she saw me lying. It's a fair enough question, but I don't have a sensible answer for her.

'Just old friends,' I say. 'Quick, let's go.'

'I swear they were the guys who bought all that expensive garden furniture today. Your friends have good taste.'

'Yes,' I say noncommittally.

'They're coming to collect it on Saturday before they move into their new house.'

'Good for them,' I reply. 'Now then - let's get going. Shall we try The King's Arms?'

'Sure,' she says, crunching the gears as she moves off and heads towards the pub. Once we arrive in the car park, she parks her car very badly, taking up two spots by parking on the dividing line between the Then she blocks another two by sticking her bumper out so far that she's effectively prevented anyone from getting into the spaces behind her. Four parking spots for a tiny car? That must be some record. I feel strangely proud of the woman.

We walk into the pub, order wine, and sit in a corner booth. We clink our glasses together.

'To Christmas,' says Belinda.

'Christmas.'

'I hope you didn't mind me asking you to come out tonight. I know you must be busy with all your amazing, valuable work,' says Belinda. She talks about me as if I'm running the Red Cross.

'Don't be silly,' I say.

How much work does she think it entails to string up some lights and make a post-box out of cereal packaging?

'It's just so hard to know whom you can talk to. You always seem so professional and on top of things that I thought you might be able to help.'

This is not a common description of me, so I pause for a while to cherish the flattering words.

'I'm delighted to help,' I tell Belinda. 'Honestly, anything you tell me will be in confidence, and if there's anything I can do to assist or make life better at work, you only have to say.'

'No, this isn't at work,' says Belinda, and I regret that I feel a pang of disappointment.

'It's embarrassing, but it's my mum's boyfriend. He keeps telling me how much he fancies me, and I'm unsure what to do about it.'

'Oh no, that's awful. I'm so sorry,' I say. 'That's a tough situation. I'm sorry, but I thought you meant one of the guys at work had been coming on to you, and I was going to suggest all sorts of things, but it's a bit harder if it's in your home.'

'Yeah, it's tough.'

'Weird but harmless,' I say. 'Tell me a bit about this awful boyfriend, and I'll see whether I can help. Has she been seeing him for long?'

'Just a couple of months, and I don't like him. And he's now become a bit, you know, affectionate. Is that the right word? He strokes my hair when he walks past me, telling me how lovely I look.

'Mum smiles when he does it, she thinks it's great that we're all getting on. But we're not all getting on well at all. I'm certainly not getting on well with him. I'm sick to the back teeth of being touched by him.

'Then he got drunk last night and told me he fancied me. I didn't know what to say.'

'Tell him to piss off, and you tell your mum straightaway. Honestly, you don't have to put up with all this. Don't let someone in your home make you feel scared and uncomfortable.'

'But I don't want to upset mum.'

'I promise you; your mum will want to know. And she needs to know what sort of scumbag she's going out with, doesn't she? For her good as well as yours. If you don't tell her, you're not protecting her. On the contrary, you're leaving her vulnerable to more bad treatment from him and making your own life very difficult.'

'Yeah, I guess,' says Belinda. 'I thought that maybe I should move out or something like that. Just get away from the situation.'

'No, you've done nothing wrong. You need to tell your mum.'

'Yes, I'll tell her. I promise I'll talk to her. Thank you. I feel so much better now.'

'And, if things get terrible, call me any time. You can come and stay with me if you need to. I mean that.'

'Oh my God, Mary. Thank you so much; you are so kind. I didn't want to move out and get a place of my own: I get so lonely.'

'No, you don't have to live on your own. But - equally - you shouldn't be drummed out of your own home by this scum bag; tell your mum, and I'm sure everything will be OK. If it's not, you know where I am.'

'Thanks, Mary. Do you live by yourself? I did it once and hated it.'

'I have my place on my own, but my boyfriend Ted is always around, so I never get lonely.'

'I'd love to have a boyfriend,' she says. 'It must be amazing to have someone there who loves you, no matter what. And you can tell them anything. And everything's lovely. You have this gorgeous perfect man at home, waiting for you.'

I get the sentiments of what she's saying. But when I think of Ted scratching his balls and picking his nose, the words 'perfect man' don't spring quickly to mind.

'How did you meet Ted? I don't know how to meet anyone. I've never really had a boyfriend.'

'I met Ted at a club I went to.' I don't want to tell her we met at Fat Club, so I tail off before explaining what sort of club and offer her advice instead.

'I think your best bet is to get out as much as possible. You will never meet someone in your house, so you need to join clubs, even go to the gym if you can bear it. I know it's one of the most dreadful places on earth, but it is full of men. Or even go to a cafe, sit, drink a coffee, and look around. You know you can go to many places where you might meet someone. And have you tried internet dating?'

'No, I could never do that.' says Belinda. 'Honestly, I'd hate it.'

'I understand. And, to be honest, I'd focus on sorting out

the situation with your mum's boyfriend first. That's the priority. Then I'll help you find a boyfriend if you'd like.'

'Oh, that would be great.'

'OK, promise me you'll go home and talk to your mum.'

'I will,' she assures me. 'Mum and her boyfriend are away this week. They are back on Sunday, and I'll talk to her then.'

'And you'll tell her how upset this is all making you?'

'I will,' she promises, and we clink our glasses together again.

THE POSTBOX OF WISHES & DREAMS

1 6th December

My first task on this lovely, though chilly, morning is to head out to the grotto and switch on the sparkly lights and Christmas music. My original plan was to play carols, but, I'll be honest with you, I don't take much to carols. The thought of listening to 'Away in a Manger' through the second-rate music system all day filled me with horror. So, instead, I decide to play a mixture of Christmas favourites. I don't know what it says about my sophistication and religiosity, but as 'Last Christmas' bursts into life, I'm prepared to admit that I prefer Wham to choir boys.

Next, I turn my attention to the *Christmas Post Box of Wishes and Dreams*, sitting proudly before me. I open the little door I fashioned on the front of it and stick my hand inside.

Oh my God.

There are letters in there. I feel a thrill rush up through my body. I *hoped* there would be letters, but there *are* letters. I count them. There are 12 in total. Oh my God. I pull them out, tie the whole thing back down again, and disappear into the office to read them. I'm pretty good at giving advice and offering kind words; I hope I can help with these.

I sit down at my desk and open the first one.

I swear to God - some people are rude. I'm unsure whether I should tell you what they wrote, but many of the suggestions would not be anatomically possible. And the suggestions about the reindeer's antlers? Who thinks like that?

I put the rude letters to one side and discover, to my great disappointment, that there are only three left that aren't obscene.

The first of these says: 'I wish the store were cheaper.' The second says: 'I wish someone in this place knew the difference between a flat top grind saw and a triple chip grinder.'

I can't do anything about the prices in the store, but I plan to send a formal letter back to the writer of the second letter, explaining that there are lots of people here who can help with particular tools, and giving him the name of a member of staff who he can contact.

I expected to be busy all morning, writing letters and trying to find the answers to problems. I feel a wave of disappointment that I won't be able to help people in the way I thought I would. I've only got one more letter to read. So I put it to one side. I'll save that for later.

'You look miles away,' says Keith, coming into the office to see me. 'What on earth are you thinking about?'

'Rude men, chip grinders and flat-top saws.' I say.

'Not more mad things to go in the manger with the elephants, I hope.'

'No, and elephants have a legitimate place in the manger.'

I'm going to open the final letter. I can't wait any more. The letter sits in a pale blue envelope with neat, slanted and elegant handwriting...as if written by a quill-wielding, sophisticated gentleman from the early 1900s.

The letter inside isn't on matching pale blue paper, which is disappointing, but on plain white A4 paper instead.

Daniel.Johnson@gmail.com
Dear Father Christmas,
I wish I had a girlfriend for Christmas. I feel so lonely some-times. Can you help arrange a date for me? I am free on 20th December if that would be possible.
Kind regards,
Daniel

I TURN OVER THE PAGE, but there's nothing written on the back. No address, no phone number. I push it back into the envelope. Gosh. It's a sweet little note, and I feel a rush of desire to help, but I'm unsure how to do that. I suppose I could put a note in the centre asking all single women to nominate themselves for a date. Perhaps I could run a competition...

Win a date with Mr Lonely from Surrey?

Na. There's no way Keith would let me do that. Not in a million years.

I pull the letter out of the envelope again and look at the writing. I have such a lovely feeling about this guy despite having no idea how old he is. He could be in his 50s or 60s, but I see him being a couple of years older than me, romantic beyond his years, courteous and kind. As I ponder the situation, Bev from crucial cutting and electricals walks past and pulls a face at me through the window. I make an equally silly face back.

Then Belinda walks along and pulls a daft face at me. I pull another silly face back. We always do this. Instead of greeting one another like adults, we've all taken to gurning at each other. It's most peculiar.

Hang on.

Belinda is keen to meet someone.

Daniel and Belinda.

That would be perfect.

'Belinda,' I say, rushing out of the office, clutching the letter in my hand. 'Stop for a minute,' I shout. 'I have something to ask you.'

I catch up with Belinda, who has caught up with Bev, and they both stop and turn round as I charge towards them with all the grace of a stampeding rhinoceros.

'Look,' I say, brandishing the letter at Belinda. 'Read this letter.'

Belinda reads it and looks up at me. 'Wow. He sounds nice. But what does he look like?' she asks.

'Well, that's the problem. I've no idea.'

'Is he my age?'

'I don't know that either. It's just come...it was put in the *Christmas Post Box of Wishes and Dreams.* Do you want me to investigate further?'

'Does he live nearby?'

'I guess so,' I say. 'He must live fairly near, or he wouldn't come to this centre. And look how neat it all is. He must have seen the post box going up yesterday, gone home to write a letter, and then returned to post it. So I imagine he lives near. If I can find out, would you like to go on a date with him?'

'Er...yes,' she says. 'I mean - yeah, why not. Just make sure he's not, like, 60 or something.'

'Yes, of course,' I say. 'So - you're sure? I can go ahead and plan it.'

'Yeah - what the hell. It's Christmas, and I've had a shit year. So go for it, girl, and let me know where we're going.'

'Great. I'll contact him now.'

'Just make sure he's not too old,' shouts Belinda as I walk away. 'I don't want to date my Grandfather.'

'I will. Are you free on Saturday?'

'I am at lunchtime,' she says.

'OK, I'll try and arrange something for Saturday lunchtime.'

Dear Daniel,

Thank you so much for your letter in the Christmas Wishes Post-box. I'm sorry to hear that you feel lonely. We'd love to set up a lunch date for you, with a lovely girl, here in the DIY centre on Saturday 20th at 1 pm. Do you have a picture that you could send us? Also, I hope you don't mind me asking this, but are you under 40?

Thanks very much, Mary 'Christmas' Brown.

It's just minutes before a reply is forthcoming.

'Thank you. Yes, I'm under 40, and I would love to go on a date.'

No photo, but as long as he's under 40, that'll be fine. Belinda's lovely, but she's not going to win Miss World anytime soon. I know that sounds cruel, but all I'm saying is that looks aren't everything, and if he's in the right ballpark, age-wise, I think we should give it a go.

I email Belinda confirming that the date is on Saturday, and I send a quick email to Keith to tell him about it. He sends a reply to say that he's at lunch, but it sounds interesting. Are there any PR opportunities through it?

'Of course,' I reply.

THE HOT DATE

y the time Keith returns from lunch, I've created a multi-dimensional PR campaign that would rival that of any political strategist. It may not look like an era-defining document...I've just put bits of A4 paper and Post-It notes together. But don't let the unsophisticated look of the thing detract from its power. This pile of papers is designed to impress.

'What the hell's that?' asks Keith, peering at my life's work as if it's something I've picked out of the bin.

'It's a PR campaign to tell the world about the great Christmas stuff we've got here at the store.'

'What great Christmas stuff? You've put up some lights, Mary, and they look great, but it's not exactly Lapland. I don't think the press will be interested.'

'I've done more than just lights. There are loads of things going on.' I feel wounded. Has he not been out there? 'There's the letterbox to send wishes to Santa's elves, who will answer all of them - except the rude ones. And there's the grotto and all the trees with wonderful decorations. And there's the nativity scene.'

40

'A nativity scene with a bloody elephant in the middle of it.'

He throws his hat and scarf onto the hat stand, and they miss the pegs, slide down the coats and land on the floor. He shakes his head as if it's the fault of the hat and scarf and stomps over to pick them up.

'I'm not criticising anything, Mary. I gave you a small budget, and you've done a sterling job, but I don't think it's a story that the global media will be interested in.'

'Yes, but the date will be.'

'What date?'

'Did you not see the email I sent you?'

'Yes, but I've forgotten now. I've been out with my wife trying to pick carpets, and I don't care what carpets we have. And now I've wasted my lunch break comparing duck egg blue Axminister carpets with seafoam-coloured Wiltons, and I'm fed up.'

I pause for a moment while Sharon brings him his coffee which she puts on the edge of his desk. Keith then swings his legs up, and I swear to God, I think he's going to kick the scalding coffee all over her. We both gasp.

'I know what I am doing,' he says. 'My feet weren't anywhere near the coffee cup. Now, tell me about this date. What's that about?'

'OK,' I say. 'Well, a lonely man put a note into the *Christmas Post Box of Wishes and Dreams* to say that he'd love to meet someone this Christmas. It was a sweet note in which he said he gets lonely sometimes, so I thought it would be a great idea if we fixed him up with someone.'

'And who, pray, are we planning to fix him up with?'

'A member of staff who is single and keen to meet someone. She's lovely, and she's lonely too. So I was going to organise a date to fix them up. A date here in the centre, in the grotto. A Christmas love story. On Saturday…this Saturday, the 20th.'

'Oh. That sound doesn't sound like a bad idea, Mary. Who's the female on the staff?'

'It's Belinda.'

'Oh.'

There's a short silence while I wait for him to say more than 'Oh,' but he doesn't, so I carry on.

'I think it could be a lovely story. It will bring attention to the Post Box of Christmas Wishes and Dreams and all we're doing at the centre to make Christmas as special as possible for the community.'

'Yes, that's wonderful. I love it. I'm just wondering about Belinda as the date. Do we not have anyone a bit - you know - more attractive? A bit thinner?'

'Belinda's lovely,' I say.

'Yes, I've no doubt. I'm just thinking about the photographs and the centre's reputation.'

'What?'

'Oh, it doesn't matter. I think that if possible, we should get someone pretty. Someone photogenic. How about Selina? She's a lovely attractive girl.'

'Yes, she's also engaged. Belinda is perfect.'

I can see Keith is still thinking, casting his mind through all the more attractive women on the staff.

'I'll get on with setting it up then. I thought we'd do it here in the centre. We can decorate the pagoda with the flowers from the cut stems department and bring out the lovely gardening furniture and make it gorgeous, and a big advert for everything we sell in the store.'

'Oh, that does sound like a good idea. Very well - you plan it all and keep me briefed. Is Mandy single? She's a nice-looking girl.'

'I don't know, but Belinda is keen to go on this date.'

'Very good,' says Keith, picking up his phone. 'Make sure we look good. And stop calling it the *Christmas Post Box of Wishes and Dreams*. It's just a Christmas Post Box.'

'We'll look good. Don't you worry,' I say to Keith, rushing off before he can change his mind.

I need to get cracking and organise this quickly because I'm due to finish work at 3 pm after coming in at 7 am this morning. Mum's coming in after work to take me Christmas shopping which I'm looking forward to, but it means I have to leave on time, no staying late to get things done.

I open a new word document on my computer... OK, so - what are the issues?

I know that Keith will baulk at us spending too much money on this date, so we'll have to get an excellent takeaway or something for them to eat. There's a lovely Lebanese restaurant in Hampton Court; I'll email them now. Perhaps they will give us a discount if I tell them about the publicity.

The decor should be easy enough to do since we're in a store full of lovely gardening furniture and flowers. I wonder whether we could get a snow machine? We could have people dressed as angels and snowflakes so the whole thing is white, sparkling, and beautiful. I jot all this down. Next, I send out press releases, inviting local journalists to meet the lucky shopper who is invited on a magical Christmas date.

It's going to be perfect.

GINGER WINE & GOSSIP

I see mum wandering through the garden centre at around 2.30 pm; she's dressed nicely but clutching a carrier bag. What is it with mums and carrier bags? I've lost count of the number of handbags I've given her as presents over the years, but she still brings a carrier bag because she wants to keep the handbags for best.

'This bag's just fine,' she says, indicating the aged Sainsbury's carrier bag she has wrapped around her wrist.'

'I want you to have nice things and use them,' I tell her. 'There's no point having them if you don't use them.'

'OK, I promise I will,' she says.

'Now come and see the decorations.' I hug her and lead her in the direction of the nativity scene.

I'm happy to say that she's impressed with what she sees. 'You have done very well there, dear. The way you have done those lights is wonderful. And the trees with all those amazing decorations! You do have a magical way with colour.'

This is another thing about mums. They can be desperately nice about you even when you've created what is a complete eyesore to all other people.

'Thanks very much,' I say. 'What do you think of the nativity scene? Don't you love how the children sit around looking at it?'

'Yes, yes,' says mum. Then she goes quiet.

'What's the matter? Didn't you think it was great?'

'You know that I think everything you do is great,'

'But...'

'Oh Mary, you know I don't like to criticise, but I was surprised to see an elephant there. I've never read a bible story about an elephant in the manger.'

'Not you as well.'

'What do you mean?'

'Everybody is telling me that there was no elephant there. But you look back at the Bible. The three wise men arrived on an elephant, a camel and a horse. That's how they got there.'

'Well, in every Christmas card I've seen and every nativity I've watched, the wise men come on camels. It's that part of the world. The part of the world with camels.'

'Yes, but one of them comes on an elephant. You flick through your bible when you get home and check.'

'I will,' she says.

We leave the centre and catch the bus to Richmond, where we wander through the shops, picking up bits and pieces for presents. I find a giant chocolate 'T' covered in marzipan, with nuts sprinkled on the top, to put into Ted's stocking. Then I pick a second one up because I know there is no way on God's good earth that I will make it to Christmas without nibbling on it.

'You should get one for dad,' I say. 'He loves marzipan, doesn't he? He always picks it off the top of the Christmas cake, which annoys everyone.'

'Oh Mary, that's an excellent idea. You're right. He does adore marzipan.'

She picks up the T.

'But dad's name doesn't begin with T? Why would you pick up a T?'

'I don't know. Why did you pick up the letter T?'

'Because Ted's name begins with T.'

'Oh yes, I see what you mean.'

I pick up some lovely earrings for the girls, in Zara, and some other bits and pieces, like a hot water bottle in the shape of a zebra and a pair of gloves that squeal when you clap your hands. Honestly, it must be fabulous being one of my friends at Christmas. Who wouldn't want to wake up to a pair of gloves squealing under the tree?

'Come on. Let's go and have a drink. It is nearly Christmas, after all.'

'Sure,' I say, because - who'd say no to a cheeky afternoon drink? But it's most unusual for mum to suggest alcohol, let alone before 6 pm.

We wander into a bar packed with Christmas revellers, many sporting their finest Christmas jumpers. In the corner, a group of people sits down to a proper Christmas meal. At a guess, I'd say it was a work party, and the people there seem to be at various levels of drunkenness. There is a relationship between how drunk they appear and how much fun they are having. The sober-looking guys glance at their watches and wonder when they can get back to the office and away from all the forced jollity while their more inebriated workmates throw tinsel at one another and smile an awful lot.

'What do you fancy drinking?' I ask mum.

'Whatever you're having, love,' she says.

'No. You choose what you want. Don't just have what I'm having.'

'I don't know. Your father gets me a glass of wine, but I'm not that keen on wine, to be honest.'

'What do you like?'

'I like ginger wine, but it makes my cheeks bright red...ginger always does that to me. I enjoy it, though.'

'Sit down, and I'll get you a ginger wine.'

The barman pours the glass of Stones ginger wine, and it's such a tiny amount that I tell him to make it a double and decide to have one myself.

Mum has sat herself down on a long table next to a rather drunk-looking man with three pints in front of him. I must be honest - it's the last place I would have sat. I'd rather be next to the festive-jumper-clad work group or the old guys sitting at the bar with no tinsel or decoration. But a man sitting on his own at lunchtime with three pints in front of him? He's going to start talking to us, isn't he?

I sit next to mum and put her glass in front of her, moving my eyes towards the old guy in the coat as if to say to her: 'why are you sitting next to him?'

'I thought he might be lonely,' she mouths back at me. Bless her. We can't even come for a Christmas drink without her trying to help someone out.

I smile over at the man.

'You're wondering why I have three pints in front of me, aren't you?'

'I thought you were probably just thirsty,' says mum, taking a large gulp of her ginger wine. Her cheeks turn bright pink straight away. It's amusing to watch.

The man, meanwhile, takes a sip of one pint, then the other pint, then the third pint. 'I bet you are wondering why I'm drinking them like this, aren't you?'

'Not at all,' I reply.

But he's not put off.

'I have three brothers: one lives in Australia, one in China, and one in the States. We can't be together this Christmas, and it's the first Christmas since our parents died,' he says.

'I'm sorry to hear that.' I take a large gulp of ginger wine and feel my cheeks flush.

'Oooo - it's happened to you too,' says mum, with a giggle. 'Your cheeks have gone pink.'

I touch my cheeks lightly as our new friend continues with his story.

'We made a vow to each other that at Christmas, all four of us would go to bars in our respective countries and drink together. So, my brothers have four Guinness Stouts too, and we're drinking together - all four brothers.'

'I can't help but notice that you only have three pints in front of you, but you said there were four of you.'

'Yes, but I'm not having one...I've given up drinking,' he says.

There's a short pause before he collapses with laughter, banging his hands on the table and creasing over with joy.

The guys at the bar laugh too. 'You've given up drinking, so you only have three pints. It works every time,' they howl.

'Come on, drink up,' I say to mum. 'We're getting out of here.'

The man continues to laugh to himself, raising a glass as we leave the pub.

'Do you think that man has sat in the pub all day, with three pints in front of him, ready to crack that joke?'

I say to mum. 'Because if he has, he's having a dull Christmas.'

'You know, I think he probably has, the daft fool.'

We leave the pub, and mum looks down the busy street. 'I'm going to head back. I've left your father on his own for too long. You know what he's like if I leave him. He'll start putting on old John Wayne films. He needs me there to keep him in order.'

'No, don't go home yet, come with me. Dad will be OK. If the worse thing he's going to do is watch old cowboy films, I'm sure he'll be fine for another couple of hours.'

'I suppose so,' says mum. 'What shall we do then? Look for another pub?'

'Have you got a problem or something? Shall I find you an AA meeting?'

'No, but that ginger wine was nice, wasn't it? I must remember to get us a bottle for Christmas.'

'Good thinking,' I say. 'It does give us both very pink cheeks, though. If we drink too much more, we'll look like beetroots.'

'Look, there's a bench here; let's sit down while we work out what to do.'

I forget that mum's getting older. It wouldn't have occurred to me to sit down, but I guess you get tired when you're over 60. I can't stand the thought of mum and dad getting old.

I take them for granted, but they're my biggest supporters and fiercest allies. They mean the world to me.

I sit on the bench next to mum and smile at her. 'Shall we find somewhere a bit nicer than a pub? How about we find somewhere where we can get afternoon tea and ginger wine?'

'Oh, that would be lovely, dear. But where?'

'I guess one of the hotels will make afternoon tea. Let me check.'

I google the hotels in Richmond and discover that the Hill Crest hotel, about five minutes from where we're sitting, makes lovely cream teas. They look delicious in the photographs. If we add a couple of glasses of ginger wine, we'll have the perfect spread.

'I've found somewhere,' I say to mum. 'There are gorgeous cream cakes at this place.'

We walk up the hill to the hotel, but it turns out it's quite a steep hill and quite a long way. Google lied to me. It's not a quick 10-minute walk but an urban route march. I try not to look like I'm struggling as I power along, carrying all the bags because I am worried about mum being old and not wanting her to be in pain or anything.

Finally, the beautiful old hotel hoves into view.

'Oh, this is lovely,' says mum. 'Worth the 40-mile hike up the hill.'

'Yes, it was a bit of a journey. But you're right…this looks amazing.'

'We'd like cream tea for two,' I say to the smartly-dressed waiter'.

'And we'd like two glasses of ginger wine as well,' mum says.

'Of course, ladies. Follow me.'

He leads us into a beautiful room with breathtakingly high ceilings and enormous chandeliers that twinkle above us in the fading light.

Cream fur blankets are thrown across the back of the seats, giving the whole place an air of comfort and homeliness, despite its extravagance. Next to our table is a beautiful Christmas tree with just a few white lights twinkling at us.

'Their Christmas trees are nothing on yours, love,' says mum, loyally.

'They haven't even got 100 Rick Astley faces on the trees. Rubbish!' I say.

'Good afternoon, ladies,' says a smartly-dressed waiter. 'I understand you would like the afternoon cream tea?' he says.

'Oh, yes, please,' says mum.

'And some ginger wine?'

'We definitely want ginger wine,' says mum, even more effusively.

'Of course. I'll be back very soon with your wine. In the

meantime, perhaps you'd like to look through the various tea options.'

He presents us with a menu each, offering a variety of styles of cream tea. They all look lovely.

'I bet this will be lovely,' I say.

'I bet it will,' says mum. 'I love you very much, Mary. And I'm so proud of you. Christmas will be such fun this year with you and Ted joining us. Just thinking about it makes me so happy.'

'I love you too, mum. And you're right...Christmas is going to be lovely.'

Shit.

A KID CALLED OLIVER

1 7th December

By the time Keith makes it into the office the following day, I'm an utter wreck. I'm lying across my desk sobbing uncontrollably. I can't stop.

'Good lord, woman, what on earth is wrong with you?' he says, displaying all the sensitivity and kindness I've come to expect from him.

He's not a man to deal gently with emotional outbursts. To him, every sign of feelings is a weakness that needs to be stamped out.

'It's one of the letters,' I say to him, gasping between sobs and trying to get the words out. 'A young boy. He's only five, and his dad has written to the *Christmas Postbox of Wishes and Dreams,* saying how much he wants to go to Lapland. He was born with one leg and has this horrible illness that will probably end up killing him in the next few years, and there is a photo, and he's gorgeous. Look at him. He's been through so much and has had so many awful operations. We have to send him to Lapland. Look, Keith. Look at him...'

I thrust the picture of the beautiful blonde kid in front of Keith. The child has wide blue eyes and a soft, gentle smile.

Keith looks at the picture and grudgingly admits it's all rather sad before saying: 'That's life, girl. I'm afraid there's a lot of shit around.'

'I know, I realise that. But we have the opportunity to help one child and make life just a little bit less shit for him and his family. Can the company pay for him to go? It would be such an amazing PR opportunity.'

'Yeah right, it's been so tight this year they won't pay for anything, let alone thousands of pounds to send a kid to Lapland. Do you know how much of a struggle I had to get the bathroom section painted? I had to fill in 45 forms for that.'

'Can we try? Please let me contact them and explain how wonderful this would be for us.'

'Send me an email with the details and all the likely costings, and I'll forward it to head office. But don't get too hopeful; the chances of them being willing to foot the bill are about as likely as the chances that one of the three wise men came to Bethlehem on the back of a bloody elephant.'

'Well then, there's every chance they'll say yes because there is no doubt in my mind that one of the three wise men did come to Bethlehem on an elephant.'

I switch on my computer to find out how much the trip will cost.

Ideally, we'd go on the 22nd of December, five days from now, and come back on the 24th of December.

I look down through the figures.

Blimey.

I wasn't expecting it to be cheap at this time of year, but I'm shocked by the cost. I go back into the search engine and suggest going on the 23rd, staying one night and coming back on the 24th. It's marginally cheaper, of course, but still recklessly expensive. The best part of £5k. Shit. Keith is never going to go for this.

Still, I need to try. So I put an email together with all the figures and a summary of why this would be such a lovely thing to do. I include details on how much promotion the shop would get.

Dear Keith,

As you are aware, we had a charming letter appearing in the Christmas Post Box of Wishes and Dreams this morning from the father of a young boy called Oliver, who was born with a degenerative disease and only one leg.

He is a happy, friendly boy who loves Christmas, and the father's wish is for them to be able to take little Oliver to Lapland.

I wondered whether the company would be willing to fund the trip. It would attract lots of positive publicity for us, and show how kind and loving we are as a company.

I have to confess that the trip would not be cheap. I've looked at the most cost-effective way of doing it, and it would still cost around £5000 to get their family of three to Lapland for a couple of days. I appreciate how expensive this is and how tight things are across the entire retail industry. Still, I think we would be more than compensated for by the incredible goodwill generated in the local community and the extraordinary publicity our kindness would bring.

If you need any more information, please do contact me.

To repeat, even though it is an expensive trip, I believe that we would have lots of marketing and PR opportunities as a result, and it would work out to be worth doing.

Kind regards,
Mary 'Christmas' Brown

I email it over to Keith, along with a picture of the child, and then I sit back with my fingers crossed, hoping that this trip can go ahead with every fibre of my being.

It doesn't take long before Keith replies.

Mary, that's just not going to happen. Is there no cheaper trip? Can we not send them to a Christmassy hotel down the road or something? Or send them one of the hampers from the seasonal goods section? If it's more than a few hundred quid, I'm not even emailing Head Office. Keith

PS Don't call it the Christmas Post Box of Wishes and Dreams.

I reply in an email, even though he's sitting a few metres from me.

But Keith, it's Lapland; it's bound to be expensive. My point is that it would be worth it. Pleeeeeease try. Please!

Keith leaves the office without acknowledging my reply to him. I see him stroll through the centre, pass my nativity scene where there's an elephant that absolutely SHOULD be in there, and off to hardware, presumably to have a sneaky fag by the exit next to the nails. He thinks we don't know, but the horrible mixture of stale smoke and mints when he returns gives away the fact that he has been smoking and that he's trying to hide it.

'There aren't huge crowds here,' he says on his return. 'Don't these people know it's almost Christmas? Mary, think of ways we can pull people in.'

'If we sent the little boy to Lapland, we'd get great publicity, and people would hear about the good work we do, and they'd come here for sure.'

'OK, Mary. Let me rephrase that...how do we get lots of good publicity without spending five grand that the company doesn't have?'

'We've got the MCD on Saturday - there's interest in that. Two local papers, Surrey Life magazine and Women Online.

They're coming. I'm sure it will show us in a great light and part of helping the community and draw people in.'

'What on earth is MCD? I thought you were running everything past me.'

'The Magical Christmas Date on Saturday. I did run it past you.'

'Oh, that. Yes, of course, you did. Well, that's good. I look forward to that. When is it again?'

'On Saturday. I'll send another press release out in the morning and see whether I can get any more interest.'

'Good, good. Well, I'll leave you to it then. And I will send off that letter you wrote to headquarters. Just in case someone there is feeling very generous, full of the Christmas spirit, drunk, or something. Just don't hold out any hope of it getting anywhere.'

'I'll call Oliver's dad back and tell him we're seeing what we can do,' I say.

'No, Mary. Don't do that, for God's sake. Just leave it until head office comes back. Don't make any promises to him.'

'Sure,' I say, but I feel sad about everything. That little boy's picture keeps haunting me...imagine being born with one leg? I need to get out of the office before I burst into tears, so I leave my desk, head past the nativity scene, and to the bench on the far side of the centre, where I often slip off to while away the hours.

Today I can't stop thinking about Oliver.

I pull the letter out of my pocket and read it once more. The words make me want to cry all over again. Before I can think straight, I have rung the number on the letter. I want to tell the father I have the letter and reassure him that I'll do all I can. I want to tell him that it's difficult, and I'm not promising anything, but I'll do everything possible.

'Is that Oliver's father?' I say to the softly-spoken man who answers the phone.

He mumbles that it is and requests that I tell him who I am.

I go through a lengthy explanation of how I'm in charge of Christmas. I hear him sigh.

'No, I'm not pretending to be in charge of Christmas around the world. I'm not claiming to be Father Christmas or anything. I'm not a nutter. I promise. I just received your letter about Oliver. I'm from Foster's Gardening & DIY centre.'

'Oh, I see. Oh yes. Right,' says Oliver's dad, sounding mightily relieved. 'I thought you were one of those people pretending to be a charity campaigner but just trying to get money out of me.'

'Gosh, no, no. Not at all.'

'You've caught me at a bit of a bad time. I'm in a hospital in Scotland with Ollie.'

'Oh, sorry,' I say.

'Yes, things haven't been great recently. It's three years since my wife died - Ollie's mum - and Ollie's not well at all.'

Oh, My God. His wife died.

'I just wanted to say that we will arrange a trip to Lapland for you and your son to go on. It would be our pleasure. I can email you later with all the details.'

'You're joking?'

'No, I'm being serious.'

'Oh, that's wonderful. Thank you so much. That will make Ollie's day. He'll be so pleased. Thank you from the bottom of both of our hearts. My name's Brian, by the way.'

'It's lovely to 'meet you', Brian. I hope that news cheers Ollie up.'

'Oliver will be delighted. I didn't know whether a store would have the budget for a trip like this.'

'Of course, the management at Foster's are very keen on helping people.'

'Well, thanks again. I can't tell you how much this means.'

'You're very welcome,' I say before ending the call and staring into the middle distance. What have I done? I mean - what in God's name have I done?

There's only one person to talk to when I've done something utterly insane…Juan. He's a nutcase who is always doing mad things himself, so he'll know exactly what to do. I met Juan on a cruise and we struck up a glorious friendship. He's planning to come over and visit just before Christmas; then, he's going to come and live with me for a while later in the year. I can't wait. I call his number, and he answers straight away.

'Ciao Bella.'

'Oh God, Juan. I've just done something completely insane. I promised a guy that he and his one-legged son could have a free trip to Lapland.'

A TREE FOR MR BECKHAM

I hear Juan giggle at the end of the line.

'No, this is not funny. It's not the opening line of a joke. This is weapons-grade stupid. I have behaved in a way that is properly God Damned ridiculous.'

'I have no idea what you're talking about. Explain.'

I hear the clink of glass.

'Are you drinking already?'

'Yes, just a little one, my lovely friend. Tell me what's going on.'

I regal Juan with the story of the *Christmas Post Box of Wishes and Dreams* and my call to the little boy's dad.

'What's wrong with that?' says Juan. 'It sounds like you've behaved perfectly properly.'

'No, Juan. I accidentally promised him a free trip to Lapland, but there is no free trip to Lapland. I made it up. Now I need to provide a free trip.'

I hear spluttering and a small cry of anguish down the phone. 'You made me choke,' says Juan. 'So there's no trip to Lapland?'

'Nope.'

'Well, that's the craziest thing ever. Why would you do that? What are you going to do? He has a disabled son...you can't let him down. You have to provide a trip to Lapland.'

'I know I do. That's what I said. But how? I thought you might have some bright ideas.'

'Fundraise in the garden centre?'

'Keith will never let me. Unless I tell him what I've done, then he'll sack me.'

'Oh, angel, I wish I was there to give you a big hug. We'll make a plan when I come on my pre-Christmas visit.'

'It'll be too late by then,' I say. 'I need a plan now.'

'OK, well - you could write to local companies asking them to donate, write to any rich individuals locally, go door-to-door collecting money. I don't know.'

'Yes. Yes. I'll have to try things like that. Oh, you've cheered me up. I feel better now...I will write to all the big companies in town, work out where the richest people live and put notes through their doors. Thank you.'

'Pleasure, my love.'

I walk over to Santa's grotto and settle myself into the big throne-like chair in the centre of it. It's cosy here. I'll have a little break; then I'll sort out getting the funding I need to send a sickly child to Lapland. So I start to relax, almost falling asleep in the comfort of the place, as the sound of Chris Rea singing Driving Home For Christmas drifts through from the cranky little loudspeaker in the corner.

'ERR... EXCUSE ME.'

I look up to see a man looking over me as I doze.

'Are you the manager?'

'Well, I'm the manager of Christmas.'

'Great. I want to buy a Christmas tree and arrange for it to be delivered.'

'Any of the guys in the gardening section can do that for you,' I say, struggling to sit up straight. 'Would you like me to take you there?'

'No, it's a bit more complicated than that. Do you mind if we talk confidentially?'

'Of course not,' I say. 'How can I help you?'

'The Christmas tree is to be delivered to someone famous,' he says.

I try to stay professional, but I feel my eyebrows raise and my mouth open involuntarily. I wonder who he's talking about.

'OK,' I say. 'We service lots of famous people here (we don't, no one famous has ever set foot in this place), so that won't be a problem. Who is the Christmas tree for?'

'It's for David and Victoria Beckham,' says the man. 'So this would need to be handled with the utmost discretion.'

Victoria Beckham. Victoria bloody Beckham.

'Discretion is our middle name here at Foster's,' I say. 'You can rest assured that we will deliver the best Christmas tree to the Beckhams and do so with every courtesy known to man.'

'Good. OK. The next question is - what's the biggest tree you can get for me?'

'Have you seen the trees we've got outside?' I say. They all seem pretty bloody big to me.

'Those out there? No, no. They are nowhere near big enough. Can you show me some that are bigger?'

'Sure, follow me,' I say, easing myself out of Santa's seat and marching through the centre to the office. Sharon is sitting there, looking utterly adorable in baby blue. She giggles as we walk in. Happily, there's no sign of Keith.

'I have a pile of booklets here,' I tell the man (I'm now wishing I'd asked him his name).

I pull out a pamphlet from *'The Christmas Tree Company.'*

'Here are some massive trees.' There's a picture of one that's so massive it looks like it belongs in a pine forest.

'That's the sort of thing,' he says.

'That is massive,' I say. 'Are you sure the Beckhams want it to be that big?'

'Yes – absolutely sure,' says the man. 'They are having a huge Christmas party at their mansion, and they need the entrance hall to look like the open sequence of every Hollywood Christmas movie you've ever seen.

'So if you can produce Frank Sinatra and have him coming down the stairs while crooning, that would be ideal.'

He laughs at his joke, but I have no idea who Frank Sinatra is, so I smile along with him.

Then I see the price of the tree. It's extortionate. 'I'm afraid that one costs £350,' I say, closing the pages.

'Very reasonable. I'll pay now,' he replies. 'It needs to be delivered tomorrow.'

'I think delivery might be an extra charge. Can I call you when my assistant returns, and I'll confirm all the details and take the payment over the phone?'

I want to run it all past Keith before going further here. I don't even know how we'd get hold of one of these enormous trees, and I've no idea how we'd deliver it.

'Okay,' says the man, standing up. 'Let's do that, but call as soon as you know. I want to get this sorted today.'

'Let me take your name, number, and the tree you want.'

'Sure, my name's Mark Hutton,' he says and starts to give me his number as Keith comes thundering into the room on the wrong side of about four pints.

'Ah, is this your assistant?' asks Mark.

'Yes,' I say as Keith looks at me quizzically.

'Oh, I'm your assistant now, am I?'

'Yes, you are. Now, Keith - this is Mark Hutton. He is here

to buy a huge Christmas tree for Victoria and David Beckham.'

'Oh my!' says Sharon, holding her face in her hands. 'David Beckham. Oh my...'

I ignore Sharon's breathless interjection and continue. 'Mr Hutton wants to order it and get it delivered tomorrow. He wants one of these huge ones.' I indicate the tree that he has chosen in the brochure.

Keith knows an exciting opportunity when he sees one, so he stops worrying that I described him as my assistant, and he gets on with writing down the code for the tree that Mark has chosen. Within minutes Beckham's assistant is placing the order.

'The delivery charge will be an additional £10,' he says.

'Sure,' says Mark. 'That's fine - money isn't an issue. I need to get everything organised.' He looks down at the bunch of leaflets. 'Do they have tree dressers in there?' he asks.

Tree dressers? Really? Do such people exist?

'What would be great would be if you could bring the tree and dress it at the house. Do you have someone who dresses trees?'

'I could do that,' I say. 'I'm in charge of Christmas.'

Silence descends on the room. It's almost as if everyone present thinks that this is a disastrous idea. Almost as if they are all thinking...she put pictures of Rick Astley all over the tree in the centre and an elephant in the manger; please don't send her to decorate the Beckhams' tree.

But Mark looks interested.

'There would be a tight brief, and Victoria has exacting tastes. Her Christmas party attracts the world's most important and glamorous people.'

'Absolutely. No problem at all. 'Tasteful' is my middle

name,' I respond, subconsciously touching the giant earrings and metres of tinsel strewn through my hair.

'OK, then we have a deal,' says Mark, offering his hand. I shake it firmly and look at Keith, who looks terrified.

'I'll just put your bill together,' says Keith, scratching his head and flicking through the brochures in front of him in a manner which suggests that he has no idea what to charge the Beckhams for the tree decorating service I've just offered. Once Mark has left, we all sit back and ponder what just happened.

'How much did you charge him for me?' I ask.

'£200,' he says. 'So I hope you're good at this sort of thing.'

'I've no idea: I've never done anything like this in my life before. I did the ones here in Christmas Land but never before that. Mum and dad would never let me near the tree at home in case I ruined it.'

DAY WITH THE BECKHAMS

'You can't do that,' says Ted, rather unsupportively.
'Yes, I can. How hard can it be? I mean - really? How hard?'

'Bloody hard,' insists Ted. 'People do proper university degrees in things like this.'

'What? In dressing a Christmas tree? What are you talking about?'

'OK, maybe not dressing a tree, but - you know - home decor and making the place look good. Isn't it normally those interior designers who do up trees and stuff, do party decorations, and make everything look good?'

'I don't know,' I say. 'All I know is that I've had the brief from the party planning company, and I've been googling 'how to decorate a tree,' and I can't see that I'll have any problem at all, so please be more supportive.'

'Sure,' he says, and we raise our glasses to the task ahead of me. I'm full of optimism and excitement; he's full of dubiousness and concern.

'In all honesty, Ted, I'm much more worried about getting this little kid to Lapland than I am about going to the Beckhams. It's upsetting me that he's having such a difficult time. I think I will pay for the trip myself out of my savings account.'

Ted smiles at me. 'You are such an incredible, kind and sweet person. I don't think you know how much I love you, but you can't pay yourself. You can't, Mary. It wouldn't be right.'

'I don't know,' I say. 'I think it might be the simplest way to get him there.'

'We'll talk about it tomorrow night,' says Ted. 'Try not to worry about it while you're doing your decorating.'

18TH DECEMBER

I rise at 7 am the following day. There's so much going on; I need to get on top. I email Belinda confirming that the hot date is on, and I send a note to Keith with a draft press release to go out to more local newspapers and magazines today. I'll send the press release when I return from the Beckhams' house tonight. I slip the letter from Oliver's dad into my bag with my savings account details. I will pay for the trip to Lapland and give the little boy the trip of his life. After we've done Beckham's tree, I'll go to the bank and sort the whole thing out.

RAY AND JOE have been tasked with accompanying me to the Beckhams, and they arrive outside my flat at 8 am to pick me up. I'm dressed and ready to go when Ray beeps the horn outside. I washed and ironed my uniform last night. I'm wearing it with just a simple white shirt underneath, and I have done my make-up in a discreet, elegant way. No tinsel, no stupid earrings, no madness at all. I'm all over this. No one needs to worry. Mary's got it under control.

'We need to go to a shop to buy the stuff to go on the tree first,' I say, directing Ray towards a boutique Christmas shop in Wimbledon, where we have identified very posh decorations that will be perfect for the Beckhams' tree. I'm aware that I will have to reign myself in here because my inclination is towards the flamboyant and fabulous, and I suspect that Posh and her friends are all about white and cream and all that understated bollocks. In fact, I know they are because of the very detailed brief I received late last night.

'Here it is,' I say as we arrive outside the shop. Ray and Joe make it clear that they are staying in the van and want nothing to do with the choosing part of the operation.

'I'm just the driver,' says Ray.

'I've just come to do the heavy lifting,' says Joe.

'OK, I'll go and have a look.' I jump down from the van's seat and waddle to the front door. You have to ring a bell to gain entry. How poncey is that? They are selling decorations, for God's sake.

I survey the beautiful interior of the shop - it looks like a jewellery shop, with the baubles laid out like they are precious jewels. Nothing in the shop has prices on it. I've been told not to worry about the cost, and to pick the best, most classy decorations, and I have Keith's work Amex card in my bag. I start to look through them...they all lovely, some of the baubles are made from shells and are incredibly delicate (I swerve those - I'm the clumsiest person alive, I'll break them if I so much as breathe on them), others have some sort of expensive sheen. They all look nice, but none of them looks brilliant. Do you know what I mean? None of them stands out or will send the guests home from the Beckham's house full of envy. They aren't right. They are expensive and elegant, but they aren't Christmassy. They are not suitable for a festive party.

'I need to think about this,' I say to the lady in the shop, leaving and walking back to the van to talk to the guys. They see me coming, and Ray winds down the window.

'Everything OK?'

'Yes,' I say, 'But the decorations are plain. I don't think they're quite what I want.'

'It's not about you, doll face; it's about the Beckhams. They like all that sort of shit.'

'I know. But I want to do something extraordinary for them. Can you come in and help me?'

Ray has lit a cigarette and has no desire to leave the warmth and familiarity of his van. Joe is on his phone.

'Mate, I know nothing about bloody decorations,' says Ray. 'I can't tell the difference between the posh ones and those tacky ones there…' he points towards the cheap pound shop next to us, and I follow his finger. That's when I see them…the absolute best Christmas decorations - bright pink with cat's faces and whiskers on them.

'OH MY GOD. I love them,' I squeal. 'They are perfect!'

'What? Perfect for the Beckhams? Are you sure?'

'I've never been more sure of anything in my life,' I say, running towards the shop as if drawn by a giant magnet.

It's so much better in this shop. Way less poncey than the other place, and the decorations are so much nicer.

I buy 30 of the pink baubles with cat faces on, and some which are shaped like pigs. Pigs flying through the Christmas tree with little curly tails that move…who doesn't want to see that on a Christmas morning? I buy tonnes of tinsel because they have it in pink, and I know that posh is all about coordination. I've seen her in Heat magazine - everything she wears matches everything else. I have bags and bags of goodies at the end. Bags bursting with pinkness. This is going to be amazing.

Then, I have a sudden thought…why don't I get some of

these for the shop as well? I pile even more into my baskets and stagger towards the cashier.

'Look at this little lot,' I say to Ray when I return to the van. He jumps out of his seat and looks stunned as he puts the dozen or so carrier bags into the back of the van.

'Bloody brilliant, eh?' I say, but he sort of half-smiles and asks me whether I'm sure that pink Christmas baubles with cat faces and pig-shaped decorations are what's required.

Er...yes. They're perfect.

We drive along in companionable silence, into the country-side and toward the Beckham's lovely country house. I can see the black wrought iron canopy leading to the front door in the distance. It looks so familiar. I feel like I've been here before, but all the research I did (mad googling last night) has made the place look so familiar. I know that beneath that canopy lies a cream and black tiled path. I can't wait to see it all.

But when we pull up at the gates and ring the intercom, there are problems.

'You can't come in,' says a haughty voice. 'We are having difficulties.'

'Oh,' says Ray. 'We've come to deliver and decorate the Christmas tree. What would you like me to do with it?'

There's murmuring in the background and raised voices, then eventually, the gates open, and we pass through them and head up the driveway towards the house. I'm so excited. I can't wait until she sees the tree when it's all decked out. She will love it, and the two of us will instantly become best friends and probably go on holiday every year with Ted and David.

Fantasies about David and I frolicking on a sun-drenched beach are bouncing through my mind as we pull up in front of the palatial abode, and I shuffle towards the door, preparing to wrap Victoria in a warm embrace. But there's no Posh Spice to greet me, just a large, Polish-sounding lady. She apologises profusely for not letting us in at the gate earlier.

'There is misunderstanding. Problems are here. Harper is bad girl today. Mr and Mrs Beckham are not happy. They are very upset.'

'Oh, I see,' I say. 'Sorry to hear that. Are we OK to come in now?'

'Yes, must come through,' she says, ushering us both into a hallway that is every bit as spectacular as I hoped. It has a wide staircase in the centre, featuring a large window on the landing halfway up, giving a fantastic view of their magnificent garden.

From a distant room, I can hear the sounds of a young girl screaming and stamping her feet in a tantrum.

'You can go in there,' says the Polish lady, pointing to a side room. Ray, Joe and I wander in sheepishly and are introduced to three party planners - all painfully thin, dressed in identical black outfits, and looking very sombre. It becomes clear that they are fed up because they want to be the ones dressing the tree. My arrival has come as something of a shock to them. They think that, because they are responsible for all the other aspects of the party, they should be responsible for dressing the tree, so everything is coordinated.

What is also clear is that I have been billed as the ultimate Christmas expert and the woman who will make the tree look amazing.

'I hear you've done this a million times before.' says the tallest of the women. She has sleek brown hair in a razor-sharp bob and the shiniest, most pointy boots I've ever seen.

'Your boots are lovely,' I say, quite mesmerised by them.

'Thank you,' she replies, and I seem to have escaped without having to answer her question.

'Do you think you should tell them that you've never

done anything like this before,' whispers Ray. 'I mean - look around you - everything is white and cream. There's no pink anywhere.'

'Just relax,' I say. 'Don't worry about a thing.'

While Ray, Joe, and three gardeners go outside to bring in the tree, the party planners help me to bring in the bags of decorations. We put them all down in the hallway, and I begin to unload the bags.

'Holy fucking Christ, are you joking?' says the older woman in the group. I think she's probably in charge. She is the prettiest, with lovely auburn tumbling curls and a perfect creamy complexion.

'How do you mean?'

'I mean...flying pigs? Flying pigs? Do you know who's coming tonight? Everyone from Elton John to the Home Secretary will be here.'

'Yay! Elton's going to love the pigs. And the cats. Look at these,' I say, pulling out the cat baubles while waving them around and meowing. 'Great, aren't they?'

There's silence from the three women, all of whom are staring at me as if I've grown an extra head.

'This is unimaginably horrific,' said razor-sharp bob woman.

'No, it's not. They're lovely. Look,' I said, wiggling the pigs in the air and making 'oink oink' sounds. 'It's going to be lovely. I promise you.'

'We're going to find Victoria,' says the third woman. She's very tall and skinny with quite a harsh angular face. Her legs are so incredibly thin they look like they might snap.

Once the women have gone, we get the tree into place. I decide there's no point waiting for them to return. I might as well get on with the decorations, so I climb onto a step ladder and begin making it look fantastic...and - my God - it does. It looks brilliant by the time I've finished. It screams

'Christmas'. I have lined all the little pigs up so they are chasing each other around the tree. They all have lovely prominent snouts. Honestly, it's the best tree ever.

In the background, I can hear the party planner women coming back. Posh is with them. She's much prettier than she looks on television. She has a natural softness about her and these enormous eyes. I decide I want her to be my best friend.

'Oh my God, Oh my God,' she says, her hands flying to her mouth as she looks at the tree.

See, I knew she'd love it.

I wonder whether she's spotted the giant pig on the top. (I forgot to get a star...I can't think of everything).

Then she starts shouting.

'This is the worst day of my life,' she says. 'It's all I need with Harper playing up all morning. Nothing will stop her from crying. This is the worst Christmas ever. Can you all get out of my house.'

'Me?' I say, looking at her with disbelief. 'You want me to go?'

'Yes,' says Victoria. 'Just go before I call security.' The sound of Harper's wails fills the room. She sounds distressed.

'Oh God, this is unbearable,' says Posh. 'I just can't stand this anymore - a screaming child and a ridiculous, cheap, nasty Christmas tree.'

The three party-planning women glare at me as she speaks.

'But it's lovely,' I try. 'It's different and fun and....'

As I speak, Harper stomps in, tears streaming down her face and anger and frustration written into every pore. Then she looks up, sees the tree, and is mesmerised.

'Ooooooo,' she coos. 'It's so lovely. Is it for me?'

She has finally stopped crying. She wipes away the last of the tears as she stares up at the tree, delight replacing the sadness on her face. Then she smiles the most enormous smile. 'It's the best thing I've ever seen in my life. Thank you, mummy.'

Harper throws herself into her mother's arms, takes Posh by the hand and leads her to scrutinise the tree. 'See the piggies,' she squeals.

Posh turns round and smiles at me. 'Thank you,' she mouths, as the party planners almost faint from the shock. 'You're a star. This is amazing.'

I'm sure you'll agree that it is a clear victory for the fat girl and her gaudy candyfloss pink decorations against the very skinny ladies in black.

FLOWERS & FAME

$\mathcal{M}$y unexpected triumph earns me hugs from Harper and a warm handshake from Victoria, who apologises for her earlier sharp words, and tells me that the peace I have brought to her house is very precious to her.

'I am a peace giver,' I say, because I'm enjoying all this love, and I don't want it to end.

I shake hands with everyone, even the horrible party planners, and am preparing to leave their lovely house when I hear a familiar voice behind me. I turn round to see David Beckham standing there. 'Cup of tea?' he offers.

Good God, he's handsome. He's not just good-looking, with nice hair, nice clothes and a sound body. He's properly gorgeous. His face is captivating, with those high cheekbones set in a well-defined jaw and perfect skin. His teeth are all shiny, and his eyes are all sparkly.

'Tea?' he asks again, and I realise I've just been staring at him.

'Oh, yes. Tea. Lovely. Please and thank you,' I say, stupidy.

David turns to look at Ray and Joe. 'Would you like one?' he asks, but my two assistants have lost the power of speech in front of the famous footballer, and they stand there, staring ahead like they are on some psychotic drugs.

'No?' says David. 'OK, well, we'll be through here, in the kitchen, if you change your mind.'

I follow David into the kitchen as Harper takes my hand. It's the most wonderful feeling in the world as she skips and smiles and continues to tell me how wonderful the tree is.

'Do you have children?' asks David.

'No, not yet. I'd love to one day,' I say. 'I love kids.' And then, for some reason, I think of Oliver, the little boy with one leg, and I wonder how he got on in the hospital and whether he's OK.

'Are you OK?' asks David, but I can't answer him because I'm choking back tears.

'Hey, you look upset. What's happened?'

At that point, dear readers, I regret to say that I burst into tears.

'Oh no, have I put my foot in it?' he asks.

'No, not at all; I'm sorry,' I say, and I tell him the whole sad tale.

He listens quietly as I talk, and I tell him I've decided to pay for the trip myself.

'Don't do anything for the next hour,' he says. 'Let me make a couple of calls, and I'll come back to you.'

'Really?'

'Yes, I'll try and help you.'

Before we leave, I get pictures of David, Harper and me in front of the tree and various shots of the different decorations. I know I'll need photos for when I put together the press releases this afternoon.

Then I collect Ray and Joe, still motionless and staring vacantly at David, and I lead them to the van.

Before we head off, I have to do a quick interview with a local news reporter at the end of the road leading to the

Beckham's house. He's keen to talk to anyone leaving the house, to ask whether they know any details about the party. I tell him that I don't know anything about the party, but I know all about the tree…

'Come on, let's go back to Fosters,' I say, as Ray starts up the engine and we hit the road. We're about five minutes into the journey when one of the guys from work rings him.

'Oh, it was brilliant,' I hear him saying, 'I was chatting away to David; we got on really well. Poor Mary was a bit overawed, but I was totally cool. I think David and I will stay in touch for a very long time.'

'Really?' I say. 'Am I going to have to listen to you telling everyone how you and David got on like a house on fire?'

But before he can answer my phone rings.

'Mary, it's David,' says a familiar voice. 'I just wanted to tell you that I've sorted out that trip for you…for the little boy without a leg. A man called Michael Foley will call you this afternoon.'

'What?'

'You told me about the little boy who wanted to go to Lapland? Well, my manager has contacted a company that will give you a free trip - for the kid, his parents, you, and a guest for a few days before Christmas. And I'll come to the airport to meet him when you return. But don't tell him that bit, then it'll be a nice surprise for him.'

'Oh God, I love you,' I shout. 'You have no idea what this means. If you ever leave Victoria, please, will you marry me?'

'Well, um, I. I'm not planning to leave Victoria.'

'I know, but it was worth a shot.'

'So, you'll tell the little boy's mum and dad?'

'Yes, I will,' I reply. He doesn't have a mum, but I'll tell the dad. 'Thank you so much. Honestly, this is just wonderful. I think I'm going to cry.'

'Just a couple of conditions,' says David. 'If Harper wants

her own Christmas party in a few days, will you come back and do her tree for her?'

'Of Course,' I say. 'Yes, 100%.'

'The other thing is - could you hold off telling anyone except the boy's dad for now? I don't want any press - everyone will think I'm helping to get press attention which I'm not. If you could tell work and anyone else who needs to know after I call you in a few days when it's all set up.'

'No problem, David,' I say. 'Discretion is my middle name….'

I smile to myself. I'll go back to the office now and sort everything out - the date on Saturday, a press release about today, and the fantastic Lapland trip beginning next week. Bloody hell, Christmas is starting to come together.

THE GLORIOUS RETURN TO THE
GARDEN CENTRE

*B*y 4 pm, the story of my great success at the Beckhams' house this morning is spreading through the store like a bushfire. There have been mixed reactions to the news that the Beckhams loved my interior designing skills. Actually, that's not true - scrub that - the reactions have all been the same; everyone is GOB-SMACKED. They can't believe that I could have made such a success of it.

'I'm pleased for you but AMAZED,' says Sharon, while Ray and Bob regale everyone with the details.

'The look on the stylists' face was a picture,' they say. 'They were all there, dressed head-to-toe in some fancy designer gear, and up rocks Mary in her bloody green overalls, which make her look like Kermit, the frog, and she's twice the size of all of them put together.'

'Alright, alright,' I say. 'No need to get personal.'

'Sorry, love, but it was very, very funny.'

I can see that some of the women in the group are wild with jealousy, that I managed to pull it off. I got myself inside the Beckham's house and decorated a Christmas tree in a manner that delighted them. I know that half the people here today were hoping I'd mess up...I am determined to rub my victory in as much as I can.

'Call me Kelly Hoppen!' I keep saying. 'I'm the queen of interior design.'

We've all gathered in the giant gardening conservatory in front of the company Christmas trees that I have just done out in the style of Posh's tree.

We'll trade off the link to the Beckhams to sell as many of these trees as possible. There is a whole row of them, all with the little pigs chasing each other across them and lovely pink cat faces looking out. They are heavily adorned with tons of tinsel that I have just thrown onto them, as I did with Victoria Beckham's, to create an artistic and spontaneous look. In short, my trees look unique.

Next to them is the Rick Astley tree. The whole scene is quite a feast for the eyes.

Sharon isn't convinced. 'What was it about the tree that the Beckhams loved so much,' she asks.'I mean - I'm not being funny, but you wouldn't imagine Victoria thinking that it was very sophisticated.'

'She did,' I reply quickly. 'She thought the tree was stylish and elegant and leant a certain stylish flavour to the house.' I'm lying, of course. I'm not going to mention to anyone that I only got away with it because of the intervention of a small child.

Sharon nods disbelievingly and continues staring at my mad, pink trees.

The whole shop looks stunning today. Now there are loads of decorated trees and the nativity scene, which looks great with its elephant, camel and donkey. It's a shame that the stuffed donkey is twice the size of Joseph and looms over everyone slightly threateningly. He's also wobbly on his legs, so I've had to lean him up against the manger, which does nothing to diminish his intimidating presence in the scene.

Away from the nativity, there's a beautiful area for Father Christmas to sit and meet children - it's full of fake snow and sleighs and has Christmas music playing and the occasional jingle-jangle of sleigh bells. There are also elves and a couple of fairies (I liked them - I know they're not in the original tale, but they look cute).

Then there's the pile of presents for Santa to hand to children and the sweets and cards I've bought. It all looks great.

'Blimey, how much did this lot cost?' asks Keith. 'Did you get it all for under £250?'

'Yes, of course,' I say (no, I didn't – it was nearer £500).

'Well done,' he says. 'Well done, indeed. This is all fabulous.'

'Thank you,' I say. 'Now I should finish some work and check the Postbox of Wishes & Dreams. Hopefully, there will be lots of lovely letters in there.'

'Yeah, once again, Mary. Let's not call it that. It's just a Christmas Post Box, and you can tackle it in a couple of days. For now, relax. Don't try to do too many things at once. You're a superstar, Mary Brown; we need to look after you.'

'But I'm off tomorrow. If I don't look at them now, it'll be two days before I get to them.'

'That's fine,' says Keith. 'Enjoy your day off tomorrow and then answer the ridiculous requests from customers when you're back. I think this Beckham thing is far bigger than that damn post box you're so obsessed with.'

As we are talking, Mandy from accounts walks across the gardening section towards me, holding the most beautiful bunch of pink flowers I've ever seen in my life. It's an enormous bouquet. She hands it to me, and I lean over and kiss Keith on the cheek to thank him for them.

'What the hell are you doing, woman?' he says.

'I'm thanking you for these flowers,' I say, opening the envelope tucked into them.

'I didn't get you those. Why on earth would I buy you flowers?'

'Because I went to the Beckhams this morning and did their tree and because I made the shop look amazing,' I say, then I read out what's written on the card:

'Thank you so much for making our Christmas tree look wonderful. You are a superstar; much love, Victoria and David Beckham x.'

'Yay! Have you seen this?' I say to Keith, showing him the card.

'Bloody hell!' he says, genuinely impressed with what he's seeing. 'I don't believe you've just had flowers from David Beckham.'

'David Beckham? Really? Has David Beckham sent you flowers?' a young mother comes up to me, having overheard Keith's words. She's at the nativity scene with her son and declares herself a massive fan of the former footballer. 'Can I see the card?'

'Yes, of course,' I reply proudly, showing the greeting buried in the floral arrangement and watching her swoon before me.

Quite a crowd has gathered around me as people regard my flowers admiringly.

'Why has he sent flowers?' asks one man, smartly dressed and a little out of place among the pink trees, tinsel and toddlers.

'I went over and decorated his Christmas tree, just like that one,' I say, pointing towards the large tree in front of us. 'That's a replica of the Beckhams' Christmas tree.'

A lady pulls her phone out and takes pictures of the tree. Others soon join her, all flashing away and capturing the image of my pink, glittery tree in their phones.

'Would you stand next to it,' asks one lady, and then it feels like dozens of people are taking pictures.

You can hear the hum of general chatter in the store, punctuated with 'David Beckham...Victoria Beckham...pink tree...' as they share the information and post their news on Twitter and Facebook.

'Are you available to come and decorate my tree?' asks one lady.

'Oh yes!' says another.

Then there are lots of questions about where I got the decorations from and whether they will be on sale in the store, and I'm filled with a warm glow and a rush of excitement at the thought that flying pigs in Christmas trees are going to be ALL the rage in this affluent part of Surrey this festive period.

'We need to capitalise on this,' says Keith. 'I'm going to get onto the warehouse and order loads of decorations like these, and we'll sell them in the store. I'll make a sign: '*You too could have a Christmas tree like David Beckham.*' You're a bloody genius, Mary. You are.'

'That's a great idea,' I say. 'We could sell loads and get some of the money I spent on this place.'

'It was only £250, don't worry about it,' says Keith.

'Have you got a minute?' someone says to me. I turn around to see a small woman dressed entirely in brown.

'Of course. How can I help?'

'I'm from the Cobham Advertiser, I'm here shopping, but I couldn't help overhearing what you said. Is there any chance I could interview you?'

'Yes,' I say. 'Of course.'

There's another woman behind her; she's just arrived and is on her phone but signalling that she needs to talk to me.

'Hi, I work for Vogue magazine. I saw the trees on Twitter. We want to do a shoot here. Would that be possible?

We'd bring models and put them around the Beckham Tree for a feature online.'

'Hi, sorry - but I was here first. The interview will only take about 10 or 15 minutes, then we can get the story online in the next couple of hours, and it will be in the paper at the end of the week,' she says. 'The Cobham Advertiser, your local paper. Good for sales.'

'Sure. Fine,' I say.

'And do you mind if I get my photographer to come?'

'No problem,' I say. I look around and see Keith standing there with his thumb up.

'So, that's OK?' says the woman from Vogue.

'Yes,' I say.

'Well done, sweetheart,' says Keith. 'You go off and do the interview, and we'll talk later. Remember the party tonight - it's going to be rocking.'

'Sure,' I say. Works' Christmas party...rocking...Great!

I do the interviews, then sneak back to the office, away from the commotion in the gardening section. And there I sit, quietly smiling to myself. I'm going to be able to send Oliver to Lapland. That matters to me more than anything.

THE OFFICE CHRISTMAS PARTY

'Why are they holding the party in such an odd place,' says Ted. We have to drive over this complicated road system to get to the work Christmas party.

The junction in Hounslow reminds me of when you go over the Severn Bridge to get into Wales. Do you know the one I mean? Is there more fun in the world than when you go over that? Suddenly there are no lanes, and it's a mad free-for-all to get into a lane. I love it. Ted and I went away for the weekend to Cardiff and went over that bridge, and we were both screaming as he drove flat out on the road with no lane markings at all, fighting against all the other traffic to get to the front of the lanes when they arrived.

'Can we go back and do it again?' he asked. 'It's like Thorpe Park.'

And this bloody road system in London is just as bad...it's like wacky races, with cars shooting around us from every direction.

'Left,' I say. I'm in charge of map reading, but I can't make head nor tail of the map or the roads. It's not an ideal situation.

We finally find the place - a big hotel called 'The Fallgate'. Ted pulls over, and I jump out. He's not coming with me tonight because it's a 'no partners' party. They do this so that we are forced to mingle and can't just sit there all evening, chatting to the person we came with. It just means being stuck in a corner talking to Jed from the lighting department about bulbs and lampshades.

'I wish you were coming,' I say to Ted as he kisses me goodbye.

'You'll have more fun without me,' he replies. 'Anyway - I've got the football to watch. Call me later, OK?'

'OK,' I say as I watch him drive off, waving through the open window as he goes. I do love that man, you know. He drives me nuts sometimes, but he means everything.

I pull out my phone and text Ray and Joe to see if he's here...I don't fancy walking into the room alone and having to frantically scan faces, looking for someone I know. There are about 20 missed calls and a whole stack of messages on my phone. Christ. Every journalist in London is keen to talk to me about my experience at the Beckhams. The Cobham Advertiser interview must have gone online...now everyone knows about my Christmas tree experiences. It's like I'm famous or something. I'm unsure what to do, so I tuck my phone back into my bag and decide to sort it out tomorrow. Right now, I need a large drink and a handful of salted, savoury snacks.

In the main foyer of the hotel, there's a sign:

'The Felgate is pleased to welcome all the staff of Fosters DIY stores in the north Surrey area. We hope you have a lovely evening and a very Happy Christmas.'

Excellent, That's nice, except that the sign doesn't say where we have to go. It's nice to get a cheery festive greeting, but some directions would also be excellent.

I wander through the reception area, looking for clues.

There's no reply from the guys, and I have forgotten to bring my invitation with me, telling me which room to go to, so I stroll through the marble reception area, hoping to bump into someone I know. Just in front of me is a group of three people - all fat, middle-aged, and shuffling through towards the Queen Anne Room.

Perfect. They look exactly like employees from Fosters, and - yes - Queen Anne room rings a bell. I follow them and help myself to a glass of wine from the guy at the door. The wine is lovely...really expensive-tasting stuff. I sip at it while I wander around looking for my work colleagues, but there are so many people here it's tough to find them. A guy walks past with a tray of lovely wine, so I take another one, putting my empty glass on his tray. I'm so impressed that they have done this party properly, with a beautiful, big elegant room featuring a giant Christmas tree, but I'm disappointed that I haven't been asked to dress it. Great to have proper, good-quality wine and not the usual cheap rubbish that gets served. I might have another one. Still no sign of anyone I know, though.

'Very posh, isn't it?' I say to the couple next to me. 'And everyone looks very swanky out of their green overalls, don't they?'

They look at me the same way that one might look at an axe murderer running down the street, clutching a sharpened blade.

Then, they back off and turn to talk to someone else.

'Right - ladies and gentlemen,' says a toastmaster, resplendent in a uniform of red waistcoat and black frock coat, banging a hammer down to get everyone's attention. 'Welcome to the Christmas dinner and drinks for Parker & Parker Legal services. Please move down through the reception room into the main dining hall, where dinner will be served.'

Shit. I'm in the wrong bloody party.

'Please go through,' says the toastmaster, signalling towards the dining area. I have to admit I'm tempted to stay at this party. They don't look like they're short of a bob or two. I bet the food will be lovely - much nicer than the naff bits of pastry that will no doubt be served at our shin-dig.

'I just need to pop out to make a call,' I say, moving towards the front doors of the room.

'Of course,' says the toastmaster, opening the door and allowing me to go through. As I leave, I help myself to another glass of wine from a tray on the side. Once I'm outside, I check my phone.

'It's the Queen Mary room,' says the text from Ray. Bollocks. Queen Mary, not Queen Anne.

I get to the right place, and it's much more like I imagined it would be; plain and tired-looking with a simple pay bar in the corner...no elaborate decorations, no toastmaster and no delicious free wine.

'Here's to Parker & Parker,' I say, raising my glass and promising myself that if I ever need any legal work, they will be the firm I turn to before any other.

'OK, ladies and gentlemen,' says Keith, taking the micro-phone and looking for all the world like a low-rent comedian on a cruise ship. 'Let's get this party starteeeed.'

There are a few feeble claps from those who have both-ered to gather before him. The rest of us mill around, waiting for what will be an overlong and under-prepared speech.

'Hey, gather round,' he shouts over to us. 'We're really partying over here.'

'There you are, hero of the hour,' says Keith, throwing a cursory Christmas decoration at me for no good reason.

I'm standing next to Ray and Belinda. 'We'd better go over there and pretend to like the boss,' says Ray. 'He's standing there on his own.'

Keith's eyes light up when he sees us coming towards him. He's a nice guy. He's been an excellent boss to me over the years I've been at the company. He's just a bit...I don't know - a bit naff, I suppose. Gosh, that sounds harsh, but do you know what I mean?

'We're going to do a fun quiz,' he announces.

Those of us gathered before him do nothing to disguise our distaste. Fun and quiz are not words that have any right to snuggle up to one another in the same sentence.

Keith divides us into four teams of five people and invites us to get a chair each and assemble in our newly-formed groups to begin the fun. Since trying to organise 20 people when most of them are drunk is a little like trying to herd cats, this process takes about 20 minutes, and by the time we're all finally sitting down and ready to start, I, for one, am losing the will to live. Keith looks more exasperated than any man has ever looked before.

'Finally,' he says. 'Right - now for the quiz...can you nominate a person in each group to write down the answers.'

Again, given the level of alcohol consumption, this takes way, way longer than it has any right to.

'Come on,' says Keith. 'It's like trying to get toddlers to organise themselves.'

It strikes me that this is a pretty good analogy. Drunk people are very much like toddlers...staggering into things, unable to make it to the toilet on time, and babbling nonsensically.

Finally, we are in our groups, and Keith can start his God-forsaken, entirely unwelcome quiz. I'm with Belinda, Ray, Joe and Sandra from catering.

'OK,' he says. 'In the store, we asked questions of lots of people, and I have the answers here. You have to guess what they said. The person who gets the closest wins the prize. Does that make sense?'

'Yes,' we all chorus, hoping there aren't too many of them.

'OK, ready for the first question?'

'Yes,' we all say again, with slightly less enthusiasm. I wish he'd get on with the damn thing.

'OK. What is the worst way to start your day?' he asks. 'Would the appointed spokesperson in each team please raise their hand when they are ready?'

I throw my arm into the air before consulting with the team—Sandra voices her anger.

'Well, do you have an answer?' I ask her, and she mutters that she doesn't, so I turn back towards Keith, waving my arm impatiently.

'OK, Mary's hand was up first. What do you think the answer is?'

'Is the answer: the worst way to start your day is to wake up on the floor and discover that your Siamese twin is missing...the one with the vital internal organs. Is that the answer?'

'No, Mary. No,' says Keith, looking distressed.

'OK - in a prison cell.'

Everyone looks open-mouthed. Well, what did they expect? This is supposed to be the worst way to start your day. It's got to be something terrible.

'Dead,' I say. 'Is that the answer? The worse way you can wake up is dead.'

'No.'

It turns out the correct answer is 'having overslept' - for God's sake. That's not the worst way to start your day...I can think of loads of worst ways.

'Mary, you have a peculiar imagination,' says Simon from customer services. 'Remind me never to be alone with you on a dark night.'

'Next question,' says Keith. 'Let's see if someone other

than Mary can answer. Mary - please make your answers less...what's the word I'm looking for?...troubling.'

'OK,' I mutter, but I'm not put off; I'm in my stride now and determined that we should win this game.

'And let the others on your team contribute,' he adds. 'It's a team quiz.'

'Yes,' I say, but I'm thinking ', *fuck that...I've got a load of dimwits on my team.*'

We play for the next hour. HOUR! At a bloody Christmas party. I contemplate leaving and returning to that lovely lawyers' party on several occasions. That was so much more classy, and no one was asking stupid questions and judging you on your answers.

'OK, this one is the decider,' says Keith, now clearly losing patience with us and confidence in his own game. 'The question is - what was the name of my childhood friend?'

Marty from the kitchen department throws his hand into the air immediately. Marty is an odd-looking creature. He's extremely thin (almost skeletal). He looks like a box of KFC after you've eaten all the chicken and thrown the bones back in. He's also a terrible chain smoker in an old-school way, with roll-ups and yellow fingers to prove it.

'Was your friend called Mike?' he asks.

'No,' says Keith.

'Barry?'

'No'

'Peter?'

'No, look, Marty - you can't just keep shouting out names; you have to confer with your team and come up with an answer. 'Anyone else?'

'I know,' I say. 'Did you not have any friends? Maybe you just had an old cereal box onto which you painted a face and called it Brian the box, which became your best friend?'

Keith looks at me like I'm the most ridiculous person on earth.

'Let's end the quiz there. Everyone has won,' he says. 'Collect your free drink from the bar whenever you're ready.'

There's a free bar running between 9 and 10 pm, so this is not quite the generous gift that it might appear, but I don't want to bring this up with Keith. I've upset him somehow...he's staring at me like I'm some lunatic. Does he need to be reminded that I'm nearly famous?

Behind me, Father Christmas is saying his 'ho, ho, hos' and swigging from a beer bottle.

'Alright?' asks Neil from kitchen appliances.

'I'm fine,' I say. 'I'm just admiring Father Christmas. He's a bloody handsome fellow.'

'I'm going to make a bet with you, Mary bloody Brown. Yes - we're going to have a bloody bet, you and me...a bloody bet.'

'OK,' I say, ordering myself a bottle of wine (the free bar's only there for an hour, I need to fill my boots while I can). 'Go on then, let's have a bet.'

A DAY OFF

*T*hank Christ, I haven't got to go to work today...I took the day off to do my Christmas shopping, which was the best decision in the world: I don't think I've ever felt so bad.

I stretch out in bed and feel immediately constrained by something. I can't fathom what it is, but it's bloody annoying. I look over to see that I'm fully dressed, and my sleeve is caught on the bedstead. Strangely, I appear to be dressed as Father Christmas. Ow - and my leg hurts. Whichever way you look at it, this is not good. Questions which immediately spring to mind are: where are my real clothes? What did Father Christmas go home wearing, since I appear to have his outfit? At what stage did Father Christmas and I swap clothes, and did I do this publicly? And why does my leg hurt so much? I think Sharon from catering might be the person to ask.

I pick up the phone gingerly and dial her number. She answers straight away with a girlish chuckle.

'Mary Brown. What are you like?' she says.

'I don't know,' I want to reply. 'What am I like? Tell me.'

'So you got home safely then?' she asks, laughing again, clearly at some memory of me that she is not choosing to share.

'Home safely,' I say. 'All dressed as Father Christmas….'

'Ha,' she laughs, giving nothing away.

'I was surprised to wake up in a Santa costume,' I say, hopeful that she'll explain my outfit to me.

'Well, you took the bet,' she says.

'Yes, indeed.'

What bet? What's she talking about? I don't think Sharon hangs around too many people who get hideously drunk, or she'd know with absolute certainty that she needs to spell these things out, or I won't know what is going on.

'Well, I'd better go,' she says. 'It's crazy, crazy here today. Thanks to you, the store is packed. People are queuing to get into the car park. Father Christmas is booked up until 9 pm on Christmas Eve. It's mad. Keith says people are driving hundreds of miles to see the Beckham Tree and to buy the decorations, and there are loads and loads of journalists wanting to talk to you. They are all coming in tomorrow. I hope that's OK?'

'Of course,' I say.

'Bye,' she says, and she disappears off the line, leaving me none the wiser about the bloody outfit I'm wearing and some bet I had.

I text Neil. 'Did I make some sort of bet last night?' I ask him. A couple of minutes later, the phone rings and all I can hear is Neil guffawing and chortling. So, that'll be a 'yes' then.

'Just stop laughing and tell me what I did,' I say.

'Do you not remember?'

'Not a thing,' I say.

'You had a bet with Dom and Pete from the warehouse that you could get yourself onto *This Morning*, the TV show.

The bet was that you have to wear that Father Christmas costume until you've been on there.'

'Been on there?'

'Yeah - you either have to be mentioned by them, be on the phone to them...on air, or go on to the show, but since you have to wear the Father Christmas costume all the time, you might not want to do that.'

Oh, for God's sake.

'That's a ridiculous bet. There's no way I can do that. So why did I bet with them?'

'Because you were drunk?'

'Well, yes, that's hard to deny. How long have I got in which to get myself onto *This Morning*?' I ask.

'As long as you like,' says Neil. 'But you must wear the Father Christmas costume until you've been on there, so I wouldn't leave it too long.'

Oh FFS.

Now, if I were a sensible, rational grown-up, I'd take the Father Christmas outfit off at this stage, fold it up, put it to one side, and dismiss the whole thing as a drunken prank at a Christmas party, but I'm not like that. I've got this maverick streak in me, and once I say I'm going to do something, I make sure I damn well do it. Or, certainly, I'll give it a try. This one might be beyond even me, though. Get onto This Morning? With lovely Holly and Phil? Bloody hell.

I make myself a cup of tea and take a banana (I curse my bloody diet on days like this...no one wants to be eating fruit when they're hung over, bacon was invented for the very purpose of comforting drinkers the morning after).

I sit down, peel the banana and switch the television to ITV. As I do, my phone bleeps with a message. I take a look:

'Thank you for your order from Top Shop. Your parcel will be dispatched from our depot today.'

What order?

I go through my emails and find one entitled 'order confirmation'. Scrub that - I see three entitled 'order confirmation' - one from Topshop for three dresses (all size 10, I would be a size 20 in Top Shop clothes if they did clothes in my size), one from River Island for a pair of shoes size 8 (I'm size 5) and one for underwear from Agent Provocateur that would shame a pole dancer. Nipple less? Really? Where the hell was my mind last night? Can it be true that I sat down at my computer at midnight, dressed as Father Christmas, drunk out of my mind, and ordered 'peep panties' and 'nippleless bras'? Yes, it is.

I'm never drinking again. Never. Not ever.

There are also loads of emails from journalists wanting to interview me. I'll have to get back to them all later. My life's just a little bit out of control at the moment.

On *This Morning*, Phil and Holly are looking very serious. With her perfect hair and lovely face, the beautiful Holly makes puppy eyes into the camera lens. 'If you have been affected by drugs, call in now and talk to our experts.'

OK. This has to be my moment. I've never seen drugs, heard anything about drugs, and I don't know anyone who's on drugs, but still - I pick up my landline and dial the number. I have to get myself mentioned on *This Morning*.

'*This Morning*, Annabel speaking.'

'Hi, I was just ringing about the drugs,' I say.

'Of course; how can I help you?'

'I'm addicted to drugs,' I say, biting into my banana. 'I'd like to talk to Holly and Phil about it...on air.'

'Certainly. Can you tell me a little about your problems…'

'I've always had them,' I begin. 'Since I was a child.'

'A child? So, how old were you when you first started taking drugs?'

I can sense that the child angle is good, and she's interested in me because I took drugs when I was young.

'I first took drugs when I was four,' I say, thinking that will pique her interest.

'When you were four? Really? Gosh, that's young.'

Yep - interest is officially piqued.

'How were you introduced to them? I mean - where does a four-year-old come across drugs?'

'Mum,' I say, and there's a short silence.

'That must have been tough,' she says. 'Your mum was an addict?'

'She was,' I say. 'She made me take them.'

'OK, look, we'll put you on air in three minutes. Is that OK?'

'Yes,' I say, grabbing my mobile to text the guys at work. They won't bloody believe this.

'I'm on This Morning in three minutes!!' I text.

'So, welcome, Mary. Can you hear me? Also, Mary - can I ask you to turn your mobile phone off - we're getting some feedback from it.'

Lovely Holly is talking to me! It's so exciting. 'Of course, just doing that now,' I reply, switching my mobile off, but already I can see Neil's reply is a whole load of smiley faces, and the message 'am watching it now.'

'Would you tell us briefly what happened to you? Is it true that your mother forced you to take drugs, Mary?'

'Yes, it is,' I say. 'When I was four years old, she started feeding me drugs, and I became hooked on them.'

'That's terrible. Dr Mike joins us in the studio. Is there anything you'd like to ask him?'

The truth is that there's nothing I want to ask anyone, and I don't want to take up too much of their time in case someone is waiting with real issues to discuss. All I want to do is make sure everyone at work knows I'm on the show.

'I just want to say how difficult it is,' I say. 'And I want to urge mothers everywhere never to give drugs to their children because it ruins lives. My name's Mary Brown, and my life has been ruined by them.'

'Indeed,' says Holly, turning to the doctor in the studio to talk about my entirely fabricated life story. 'How hard for Mary. Is that something that anyone can ever come to terms with?'

The doctor explains that I need counselling and drug therapy, and I'm urged to stay on the line so they can talk to me afterwards to offer me the help I need.

'Thanks, I'm OK,' I tell the producer, and I put the phone down, stand up and remove the blasted Father Christmas costume.

'Victory!' I say, laughing to myself. 'A lovely little victory.'

CHRISTMAS SHOPPING

1 9th December

I'm not overwhelmingly proud of myself as I grab my handbag, put on some lipstick and push the front door open. Phoning a national television station and pretending to be on drugs isn't an ideal way to start the day.

Dishy Dave, who lives just below me, leaves his flat as I step out.

'Ah, glad to see you're up and about,' he says. 'I didn't think you'd be leaving your bed today.'

'Why wouldn't I be up and about?' I reply. 'I have Christmas shopping to do.'

'Well, I thought you wouldn't be up today because of the state you were in last night. Don't you remember falling and me helping you up? I'm surprised you don't have a bruise on your leg. You took a nasty fall.'

'Oh,' I reply, pleased to know where the painful bruise came from but a bit embarrassed that Dave saw me.

'You were all dressed up,' he continues.

'Yes, that's right - Christmas party. Now I better get on my way. I've got Christmas shopping to do.'

'You said last night that you planned to do all your shopping on Amazon.'

Christ - for how long did I talk to him?

'I changed my mind,' I say bluntly, offering a cheery wave as I step out onto the pavement. He is right, though; I had planned to do all my shopping online, and my drunk self was quite sure about that, but I'm fed up with ordering things and having to send them back because they're not quite right.

I'm also really fed up with all these advertising emails… I bought mum a book about woodland birds and got an email saying, 'if you liked the book about woodland birds, perhaps you'd like these….' There followed a whole selection of things like tea cosies, screwdriver kits, and children's Postman Pat dressing-up outfits. On what planet does buying a book about birds for your mum mean that you are secretly longing for a Postman Pat costume?

So, today, despite my raging hangover, I will be buying my Christmas presents the old-fashioned way.

The first shop I come across on the High Street is Argos. In common with everyone else in the world, I wonder why the shop is still going or how it ever started in the first place. Still, I go in there and wander around, thinking how utterly bizarre it is. I flick through the catalogue, and a painting set catches my eye. My mum has always wanted to learn to paint…this would be perfect… There is a mini easel, paints and pads, brushes, and all the other paraphernalia of introductory-level painting. It really would be ideal. My dad always rings me before Christmas to ask what he should get mum, this year I told him to book her a painting course, so when I arrive with this on Christmas morning, it will complete the package. She'll be delighted, and dad and I will look like superheroes.

So I write the item number onto the pad, with the tiny little pen, and take the piece of paper to the desk. This is where shopping in Argos becomes a bit like battleships, trying to work out what's on the other side of the wall.

It turns out that they do have the painting set. Bull's-eye! So I pay my money and wait in line under a blue light on the far side of the room, looking up at the screen like I'm waiting for train details to emerge on the phalanx of screens at Waterloo station.

The art set arrives, and I head off feeling very proud of myself that mum's present has been bought. I think how happy she'll be when I give it to her on Christmas Day. But as soon as I start thinking about Christmas, I start thinking that I still haven't talked to Ted properly about what we're going to do. I need to chat with him about the fact that I have accepted two lunch invitations and we must go to both, but the time never seems right.

I wander into Marks and Spencer on the way through the centre to see whether there's anything in there that would be nice for dad this Christmas.

A lady walks up to the shop assistant in front of me.

'May I try on that dress in the window, please?' she asks.

'Certainly not, madam,' I find myself saying. 'You have to use the fitting room like everyone else.'

OK, so it was funnier in my head than when I said it out loud, but - it's Christmas - time for having fun and not taking everything too seriously.

The woman scowls at me as if I've just trodden on her cat or kicked her baby while I offer a reluctant smile and shuffle away.

So, on to the big question - what the hell should I get dad for Christmas? I mean - what does anyone get their father for Christmas? It's the stupidest present in the world to buy. He won't be impressed if I get socks, ties, or cufflinks. But what else do I get?

I pull my phone out of my bag to ring Charlie and see

whether she has any thoughts. It's switched off, which strikes me as odd. I'm the sort of person who has my phone on all day and all night. I'd have to go for counselling if I ever lost it. I never switch it off. NEVER. It's so odd that it's not on.

Then I remember that lovely Holly told me to switch it off while we were filing The Morning. I switch it back on and phone Charlie.

'Hiya gorgeous,' I say.

'At last,' she replies. 'Why haven't you returned any of my messages?'

'Sorry - my phone was off in my bag; I didn't see that I had any. What's so urgent?'

'What's so urgent? Fuck me, Mary - you were on national television this morning telling the world that your mum pushed drugs on you. Your mum is frantic and is ringing me to find out what the hell is going on. What were you thinking?'

'Oh, that!' I say. 'Don't worry about that - it was just a bet I had with one of the guys in the office. Nothing to worry about.'

'Yes - lots to worry about, Mary. You're mum's going loopy. You have to ring her. Call her now, then ring me straight back.'

'OK,' I say. I didn't think anyone would twig that it was me on the television this morning...perhaps I should have given a false name, but Mary Brown is such a common name; there didn't seem to be any point.

I dial mum's number and prepare myself to get screamed at. But it's a relatively quiet, subdued mum who answers the phone.

'Why did you say those things?' she asks pitifully. 'I don't understand.'

I explain about the bet and me being an idiot and not thinking it through.

'I'm so sorry, mum,' I say when I realise how upset she's been. And because she's my mum, and because mums are amazing, she tells me not to worry and to enjoy my shopping trip.

'Don't waste all your money on your father and me - we don't need anything,' she says.

You get lucky in life, or you get unlucky in life. When it came to mums - I've been the most fortunate person in the world.

PREPARING FOR CHRISTMAS

*2*0th December

'I still can't believe you did that,' says mum, sitting in her little car with her seat so far forward that her nose is practically touching the windscreen. She wipes a small hole in the condensation that she squints through, like a nocturnal animal peering out into the light for the first time.

'Did what?'

'Oh Mary, you know what I'm talking about - when you rang the tv company a couple of days ago and told them I fed you drugs. I think there's something wrong with you some-times; I do.'

'I'm sorry,' I say for the thousandth time. 'I bet with a guy from work that I couldn't get on the show. I shouldn't have done it; you're quite right. I'm sorry, mum.'

'And what's all the stuff I'm reading about you decorating David Beckham's tree?'

'Yes, it was something I did for work,' I say. 'They bought a tree from us in the garden centre, and I went and decorated it for them.'

'Well, everyone's ringing me about it. It's been in the papers and everything.'

It certainly has. I've done dozens of interviews, and the 'Beckham Tree' continues to be Surrey's major tourism attraction, with people coming from far and wide to see it in the gardening centre.

We're quite a ridiculous sight this morning - me and mum - driving to the dump in her little car with the old freezer sticking out the boot (tied on with ropes though God knows whether they'll hold).

'I don't know the way,' declares mum. She has no sat nav, map or even the address of the dump with her. She's so bloody disorganised, but I can't complain because in that, and so many other ways...she's exactly like me. We spent yesterday evening at IKEA - bloody hell, that was a performance and a half. Mum wanted a new freezer and had decided she wanted a massive one - the size of a bloody bungalow. She was dead set on a chest freezer, but I managed to talk her out of that; I've seen many horror films in which the body ends up in the freezer and gets eaten by the dinner guests. I wanted no part in encouraging cannibalism. But she did insist on one bigger than most restaurants have. There are only two of them. How much frozen food can one couple eat?

Mum didn't want to pay to have the old one taken away...that's why we're trundling through the backstreets of Cobham with our treacherously large load, hunting for the tip. We've asked three people so far and now appear to be heading in the right direction. Finally, on the side of the road, there's a sign.

'Here, mum,' I say, confident that she won't have noticed it. 'In this entrance on the right.'

Mum swings her car down the small side road, recklessly ignoring all the oncoming traffic as she goes. As we disappear from view, there are beeped horns and shouts, and mum seems oblivious to all of them.

We pull up on the left-hand side in front of a barrier manned by four guys (no wonder the economy is in a mess - why does it need four guys to press a button and raise a barrier).

'What are you dumping?' asks one of them, like it wasn't entirely plain from the freezer sticking out of the back of the car.

'A freezer,' I say.

The man looks down at his clipboard and back up at me.

'And you are hoping to dispose of it?'

'Yes.' What else would I be doing? No - it's full of ice cream. I brought it down here to offer you all a nice tasty snack.

'You know you have to phone us in advance if you're bringing white goods, don't you?' he says.

'Who do I have to phone?' I ask.

'Environmental health department,' he says. 'They are the council's rules, not mine. I don't make the rules; I do as I'm told.'

'Do you have the number?' I ask. There's no way we're taking this freezer back to mum and dad's house. We're leaving it here whether they want it or not. The guy hands me a number, and I tap it into my mobile phone. 'And what's your name?' I ask him.

'I'm Malcolm,' he says. 'Head of refuse.'

As I wait for someone to answer my call, the phone in the hut starts ringing.

'Excuse me,' says Malcolm. 'I better just go and get that.'

He runs into the shed while I wait for the council to answer my call. Eventually, it connects.

'Hello, refuse tip, Malcolm speaking. Can I help you?' he says.

'I want to drop my freezer off at the tip,' I say incredulously. What the hell sort of game is he playing here?

'Sure, where are you?' he asks. 'You can bring it down, but there's a backlog of people waiting. Someone's already here with their freezer.'

'That's me!' I say. 'I'm sitting in the car with my freezer. You told me to call you.'

'Great, then you can come through,' he says, walking back out again and pressing a button to lift the barrier. 'Have a nice day.'

It's late in the evening, and I'm looking in the mirror, holding back my hair to expose my cheekbones and lifting my eyebrows to make my eyes look bigger. God, I wish I weren't so fat. But, you know, the thing with putting on weight is that it affects everything...not just your body. When you think about an overweight person, you think about the size of their arse, how their stomach sticks out and that they have big thighs...that's all true, but it's also the face. When someone puts on weight, it's as if someone has covered their face in uncooked dough...the features become less distinct, and the jawline less clean. There's not a pretty little face with features but a large and rather indistinctive mask. However different you look at fighting weight, once you put on the pounds, you all start to look the same. You look less like 'you' and more like every other fat person who's ever existed. At least, that's what happened to me.

I found that it wasn't just that I got bigger, but my face became a fat person's face. My clothing became that of a fat person - the voluminous dresses and elasticated waists, the retreat into kaftans, always covering the arms, never wearing anything that defines your waist. I'm just a homogenous fat person. I look like every other fat person. All thin people don't look alike, but I fear that all fat people do. No one wants to be like that.

The sound of my phone ringing in my bag distracts me from further contemplation on the state of my face. I answer it and hear the voice of one of my very best friends.

'Hello, it's David. David Beckham.'

'Holy mother of God.'

'No, not the holy mother of God,' he says. 'Though I'm flattered that you've confused us.' I can hear the laugh in the back of his voice. 'I'm calling because it's Harper's Christmas party tomorrow, and we wondered whether you were free to come and decorate the tree for her. She loved it so much when you did it for our party.'

'Of course,' I say.

'It's late notice because the party is at 3 pm tomorrow, so we'll need you here by 10 am if possible.'

'Sure, perfect. Of course. I'll be there,' I say.

'Oh great,' he says. 'Victoria thought you'd be busy with all your other clients at this time of year, being a professional tree dresser, but if you can fit us in, that would be awesome. I can also bring you up to date with all the details for the trip to Lapland.'

'Lovely. I'll see you then,' I say.

I look over at the beautiful Christmas trees; some are decorated like the one I created for Dave and Vicks, and the others have their Rick Astley bells hanging on them. I think that - yes - one can imagine how he might have confused me with a professional decorator.

David and I say our goodbyes, and I let out a significant squeal before I run as fast as my chunky legs will carry me past the nativity scene and towards Keith's office. Mike from bathrooms sees me fly past him at lightning speed and shouts: 'Oy Mary. All the kids are asking why there's an elephant in the manger.'

And you know, his question doesn't even bother me.

'That's what one of the three wise men travelled on,' I pant back as I tear through the centre like the love child of Usain Bolt and Mo Farrah.

'The three wise men did not travel on elephants - that's complete fantasy,' says Tony the Taps.

'Fantasy? Perhaps it's elephantasy,' I shout back, laughing very loudly at my joke. Indeed, so preoccupied am I with my joke that I go tearing straight into Keith, who is emerging from his office with a clipboard and two pot plants. The clipboard drops to the ground, the greenery goes one way, and Keith goes the other.

'What is the name of the lord is all the rush for?' he asks, as I apologise and help him to his feet, patting him down to get rid of the dirt until he rudely pushes my hand away.

'Why were you rushing?'

'Because David Beckham just called. He wants me to come back over and decorate a Christmas tree again. This time it's for Harper's party.'

'Holy cow,' says Keith. 'My office. Now.'

Later that evening, Ted and I are sitting on the sofa. He's watching Curb Your Enthusiasm and laughing a lot. The other thing he's doing a lot is telling me that I am exactly like Larry David. 'Honestly, Mary - look at the chaos he causes. He's like your twin brother. I mean, you're much more friendly than he is….'

'And prettier.'

'Yes, much prettier, but you create the same level of madness and chaos.'

'You mean that in a good way, right? This guy has his own tv show, so he can't be a complete clown. Perhaps I should have my own tv show?'

'Yeah, because that would work out incredibly well. Just a

brief five-minute appearance on *This Morning,* and you managed to bring your entire family into disrepute.'

'Yeah, not my best moment.'

'Are you looking forward to going to the Beckhams tomorrow? Maybe keep it quiet this time, so we don't have the entire world's media camped on our doorstep.'

'Yes, I'm not telling anyone. I'm just going to set about the job with dignity and decorum.'

'You don't seem as excited about the whole thing this time. Last time you were practically swinging off the lampshades.'

'Yeah, well, David and I are friends now. Tomorrow will be a case of two mates getting together. No drama. No excitement.'

BECKHAM-BOUND

1 8TH DECEMBER

I wake up at 5 am, and the realisation hits me like a steam train. I feel overcome with a desire to wake Ted up and tell him. 'I'm going to the Beckhams today; I screech at high volume. You know David, the guy with the tattoos, plays football, is married to a Spice Girl and is the embodiment of manly beauty? Well - that's where I'm going. Today. Right now.'

'I thought this was just a couple of mates meeting up together…no drama.'

'It's David Bloody Beckham,' I say. 'Why are you not excited about this?'

I leap out of bed like a salmon jumping the falls and hurl myself into the shower where I carefully remove every body hair. I emerge as smooth as a dolphin and slather myself in scented body lotion before I clamber into my uniform. If things get friendly with David, he'll be delighted by my soft, perfumed skin.

I do my hair and make-up, thinking about the task ahead. I feel more excited than nervous because I know what to expect. Also, the tree is for Harper's party; I think I know what she likes. I know what sort of 'look' she'll be expecting. I think I've got the measure of her.

It would help if all the arty-farty interior designers weren't there. They were a painful, sharp-edged, jealous bunch who contributed nothing to my tree artistry.

My driver for the day is big Derek. He is working with the centre on a three-week contract to help shift Christmas trees around. Sales have increased so much since the Beckham story broke that they have had to hire extra workers.

To say that Derek is excited about meeting David Beckham would be to understate his feelings. I jump into the cab next to him, and he looks at me in amazement.

'Please tell me the truth, the absolute truth. Are we going to David Beckham's house today? Tell me, really... Or is this just a wind-up. Tell me if it's a wind-up before I get any more excited.'

'No, it's not a wind-up,' I tell him. 'This is all perfectly above board.'

'I'm his biggest fan,' says Derek in a slightly scary voice.

'David himself might not be there,' I say, eager to dampen the excitement so the poor guy doesn't wet himself.

'But we'll be in his house? Where he lives? I mean... That's amazing.'

'Yes, we will be in his house, and I think Victoria will be there to meet us, and Harper – her daughter – should be there, but I'm not sure about David.'

'Do you think they'd mind if I did videos in the house?'

'Yes, they would mind. You can't do anything like that, Derek. You must bring the tree and all my stuff in and help me when I ask you to. You can't be taking pictures, stealing David Beckham's pyjamas or sniffing his sheets.'

'Okay then,' he says, pulling the van over to the side of the road.

'Why have you stopped?'

'I better take it off Twitter.'

'Take what off Twitter?'

'I put a post up saying that I would be putting up videos giving people guided tours of David Beckham's house. So I'll take him down if you don't think I can do that.'

'Shit, yes – take it down. Why would you think you could do guided tours around Beckham's house?'

'For a laugh,' he says, as he fiddles with his phone, hopefully removing the various posts he's put up. We seem to be sitting there a pretty long time.

'Have you not done it yet?'

'There are about 50 posts on Twitter, Facebook and Instagram,' he says. 'I'm just making sure that I remove them all.'

'Oh dear God, Derek, why would you think that was appropriate?'

While playing on his phone, he shrugs, eventually declaring that all the posts are removed.

'Okay, keep going straight down this road. At the roundabout, turn left, and there is a string of shops along there that sell fabulous Christmas decorations. So that's where I'm going.'

'Is that where David Beckham lives?'

'No, Derek, David Beckham doesn't live at the back of a Christmas decoration shop on a shabby old street in south London. We'll get to Beckham's house; we need to go and buy the decorations I need first.'

We arrive at the shop, and I clamber out of the van and towards the door of the beautiful shop with its pick-a-mix of decorations. For the cheap and cheerful ones, you can get three for £1, but because this is the Beckhams' house, we're going for broke and spending a whole pound on each glossy little decoration.

This is for Harper's party, so it needs to reflect what she loves in life, and I've been through her Instagram account and found that animals and bracelets feature more than anything else. That might sound like an odd combination, and I don't expect it fully encompasses all her likes and dislikes in the world, but it's what she seems to show most of on Instagram. Of course, there are also loads of pictures of her with her dad, hugging and being carried by him, and generally being a real daddy's girl, so I bear that in mind as I scan the aisles.

I go first of all to the bright pink cats with hellishly long whiskers like false eyelashes. Could anything be better? I throw ten into the baskets before spotting teddy bears to hang in the tree. They're a mixture of brown and black ones. Black doesn't seem very Christmassy, so 12 brown bears tumble one by one into the basket to nestle down next to the girlish cats. Of course, I'll pick up tinsel in a mixture of pink, lilac and white. I'm a bit torn on the white; I think pink and lilac are great, but I throw some white because it looks like snow, and I might create a snow scene for the bears to play in. Then I see some beautiful bracelets in an array of colours. The lovely thing about them is that you hang them in the tree, and then friends can come and help themselves to a bracelet that they can wear to go home. I want some of these. They've got 40 in the shop, so I throw all of them into my basket before reaching for candy canes and some sizeable Father Christmases that you hang on the tree and squeeze to hear them say 'Ho Ho Ho.'

Honestly, I'm having an absolute field day. There are huge pink teddy bears in the far corner of the shop. They are huge, but I take one to sit on top of the tree like the star of Bethlehem. Then realise that that might be too unreligious, so I take a star and figure that if the bear is holding the star and then wedged onto the top of the tree with a branch up his bottom, that will look altogether more religious.

I think I've got enough, but I'm never one to under-do things; I'd rather take too much than get there and wish I'd bought more, so I grab handfuls of singing sheep, dancing cows that jiggle and shake when you make a noise and these crabs that crawl around sideways underneath the tree going round and round with flashy lights. I've never seen anything so ridiculous, so I buy 10 of those. Armed with two carrier bags full of £200 worth of tat, I retreat to the van and tell Derek we are ready to go. He's been sitting in the van's cab while I've been choosing ornaments and has taken the opportunity to spruce himself up a bit. He stinks of something musky and old-fashioned, and his hair has been gelled back David Beckham style. It's a style that looks perfectly lovely on the former England footballer, but on big Derek, who is pushing 60, it looks less alluring.

We drive through the countryside to the Beckhams' beautiful country retreat, then through the gates and up to the house. Derek is hyperventilating. It's not ideal.

We're greeted at the door by a collection of staff who lead us through and show us where the tree should go. Derek brings it in, and I start work.

'Can you pass me the lights I brought from work? The ones called 'pulsating disco stars,' I say.

Derek rummages through the box and hands them to me. I explain how I want them to run through the tree, one on every branch.

'I brought five boxes with us, so there should be plenty,' I add.

Derek gets his ladder from the van and begins doing as I've asked. It's quite a big job, and I feel much happier now that he's fully occupied, whistling as he carefully attaches the lights I've asked him to. Everything should be OK if he's within sight and working hard. Can you imagine if he'd gone round the house, videoing the place? We'd have been bloody arrested.

I finish all the decorating in around two hours which surprises everyone. How long were they expecting it to take? Perhaps it would have looked more impressive if I'd worked slowly and made a meal out of it. Finally, I ask whether Harper is available to come and look at the tree so I can talk her through it and make sure she's happy. The assistants look at me as if I've just asked to meet the queen, but they shuffle off and emerge 20 minutes later to say Harper will be down shortly. Only a few minutes later, I see Harper, accompanied by David.

There's an embarrassing gasp from Derek, like a teenage girl at a *Take That* concert.

'Stay calm,' I mutter as he reaches for the wall to steady himself.

I step forward and say hello to David and Harper, and I tell her all about the tree...I explain that the flashing loops are bangles she could take off and keep. I show her the mad creatures running around underneath the tree and the lights woven through it.

'It's brilliant,' she says to David. 'I can't wait for my friends to see it.'

'That's great,' says the blessed David. 'You're very good at this, aren't you?'

'I try,' I say modestly.

Then I introduce him to Derek. What a mistake. I think the guy will keel over and die when David puts his hand out. Instead, Derek stares at it. Then he leans forward and holds David's hand, rather than shake it until the lovely Mr Beckham has to use his other hand to move Derek's hand away.

'I've got this envelope for you,' he says. 'It's got all the information about the trip in it. Of course, you'll also get a call from the organisers, but so you know…everything is there.'

'Thanks, David,' I say, giving him a huge hug. 'This is amazing.'

When I pull back, Derek is there, waiting.

'Hug for Derek?' he says, putting out his arms.

'You know what, I have to go now,' says David. 'You look after yourself, mate.'

THE RETURN OF JUAN

1 9TH DECEMBER

It's 6 am on a cold morning, and I am at Heathrow Airport to collect Juan. My gorgeous little friend from the cruise ship. I'm so excited to see him.

Charlie is outside waiting in the car while I scan the arrivals concourse, looking for him. As usual, I don't need to look too closely amongst all the grey suits and blue coats for Juan as he strides into view in a gorgeous bright pink silky-looking jacket and zebra print trousers. Juan struts when he walks, treating every piece of pavement like a catwalk. He is such a magnificent creature. I wish I had an ounce of his style and confidence.

'I'm here!' I shout, prompting him to swing around and give me the biggest smile as he runs towards me and hugs me tightly. He doesn't do that thing that they do in the movies, where he picks me up into the air and spins me around. He tried that once when we were aboard the cruise liner and almost broke his back, so we stick to hugging these days.

'You look gorgeous, darling,' I say, stroking the silky jacket.

117

'It was an early Christmas present from my sister, isn't it fabulous?' he says. 'She said she might come over and visit me when I come to stay later in the year. Would that be okay?'

'Oh my God, of course. It would be lovely to meet her.'

This isn't entirely true. It wouldn't be lovely to meet her because I've seen photographs of her and she's gorgeous. I could do without her swishy dark ponytail and long, tanned limbs striding around my flat first thing in the morning.

We get out of the car when we reach mine, and Charlie zooms off straight away like she's just done some drug deal. 'I've got a meeting first thing, sorry - I have to fly,' she says before Lewis Hamiltoning it down the road.

Juan and I head inside, I put my bag on the sofa and go into the kitchen to make coffee. All the while, my phone is beeping and vibrating non-stop. I know what it is; it is all the tweets and Facebook messages after yesterday's Beckham tree thing. We put together a press release yesterday afternoon and attached the picture that I took, and it was on most of the newspaper websites last night.

'Why is your phone ringing so much?' asks Juan. 'Do you want me to answer it?'

'No, don't worry. It's just because I went to decorate David Beckham's Christmas tree and all the papers ran stories about it this morning.'

'David Beckham? What? Did you decorate David Beckham's tree? Oh my God. Oh my God. Is he gorgeous? Is he bloody gorgeous?'

'Yes, yes and yes. And you haven't heard the best bit - I was going to tell you later, but I can't wait any longer.'

'What?'

'He's sorted out the trip to Lapland. He's found someone to sponsor it so that Oliver and his dad can go.'

'No way. We must go somewhere expensive for breakfast to celebrate,' says Juan. 'That's amazing.'

'I can't do breakfast. I'm working this morning, but why don't you come to the store at 3 pm when I finish, and we can go out then, have a few drinks, and catch up properly.'

'OK,' he says, 'But I want all the details then, every one of them...'

'You will have them, my love, I promise you.'

It's 7.30 before I get to work, despite my official start time being 7 am today. Keith always works nine till six, so he doesn't know when I get to the office. So I go in, switch on my computer, and check the newspapers online to see what they've said about the Christmas tree.

Wow. The photo is everywhere. Every site I can think of is running the picture of beautiful David with his cute grin, standing next to my tree. The only horror is how big I look. I know I should be glad of all I've achieved and revel in the moment of glory, but I am twice as wide as David Beckham. And he's a big bloke. I'm also half his height. I wish I hadn't stood next to him for the photo.

I've got to lose weight. Somehow. I know this is the wrong time of year for worrying about that, but as I look at myself in the picture, I feel a tear creep into the back of my eye. The only thing that distracts me and stops me from staring at the hideous sight of myself is a loud banging on the office window.

I look up to see around a dozen people staring into the office. They cheer when I look up. 'It's Mary Christmas,' shouts one, which makes me laugh.

'How was David Beckham?' shouts another.

'Wonderful,' I say.

Blimey, it's only 8 am, the doors have only just opened, and a fan club has formed. I look back at the pictures and think - yeah, I need to lose weight, and - yeah - I do look big in those, but for heaven's sake, I'm getting some things right.

So I wave at them, eliciting another big cheer and a spontaneous round of applause.

I thank them and turn back to my computer but can sense that they are all still out there, so I head into the staff cafeteria to study the coverage on my phone, unwatched by customers. As I walk in, there's a ripple of applause, and the catering staff present me with a free caramel latte and a chocolate doughnut.

Christ. Now I'm going to be three times the size of David Beckham.

I click onto Twitter to find it aglow with discussion about my tree. Of course, there are a few unkind comments and references to my weight.

I'm surprised there were any candy canes left says Gal3345 from Leeds.

Wow! Have you seen the size of the woman who decorated it? says Peter from Barnsley.

Good grief, she's never turned down a pudding, has she? says Mandy from Bath.

It's hard to read things like that about yourself. I don't know how famous people cope with the constant bickering and nastiness about their appearance. They must have developed very thick skins to cope. Even women who are, by all objective judgement, exquisite and slim are derided and mocked relentlessly. Social media is a cruel place. I close my phone and sit back. Sod them all; I will enjoy my latte and think about the good I'm done since I took charge of Christmas.

First, there has been lots of positive PR for the store, which is excellent. Admittedly I flew beneath the standard I'd expect from Mary Christmas when I honed up a popular tv show and told them I'd had drugs forced on me by my mother. But, happily, no one seems to have linked the woman in charge of Christmas and the hung-over lunatic calling tv stations.

Then there's the *Christmas Post-box of Wishes and Dreams,* through which I've reached out to the local community. Keith may have mocked the idea that global media would cover us, but even he must agree that there has been good coverage of everything we've done, and we still have the date to come here in the store tomorrow. I send Belinda a quick text to make sure she's remembered.

I've been sitting in the cafeteria for around 20 minutes when Keith bursts in and shouts, 'You Beauuuuty!' like he's cheering a goal scorer at a football match. 'The place is packed. It's bloody packed. What are you doing hiding away in here?'

'People were looking at me through the window; I was getting fed up,' I say.

'We'll close the blinds. Anything you want, ask - you're a superstar, Mary Brown. A bloody superstar.'

'I have more good news. David Beckham helped find someone to sponsor Oliver's trip to Lapland.'

'The kid with one leg?'

'Yes. I'm going too. I hope that's OK. Just for a couple of days to make sure it all goes smoothly.'

'Of course, that's OK. Of course. Anything. Anything at all. Can I get you anything?'

'It would be great if someone could go out and empty the Post Box of Wishes & Dreams for me. Unfortunately, I can't go outside, or I'll get mobbed.'

'Of course, of course,' he says, running straight outside to do my bidding. I love how he didn't even react to my description of it as the *Post Box of Wishes & Dreams.*

Keith rushes in with the notes he's found. First, there are a few notes requesting different tin sizes in the paint and suggesting that we do wider planks of wood, then there are ones from kind people wishing us all a Merry Christmas, wishing for world peace, and generally saying nice things about the world. Finally, at the bottom, there is a letter clearly written by a child.

Dear Christmas Elf,
For Christmas, I would like One. Sticks
Two. More sticks
Three. Even more sticks.
PS I really like sticks
From,
Jamie Mason, aged five.

I'm overcome with joy that there is a task here that I could fulfil. It would be no effort for me to go along tonight with piles of sticks for this young kid. And I know exactly the man to come and do it with me.

'You want me to what?' says Juan. 'I thought we would have a few beers and talk about David Beckham.'

'Yes, we will go to the pub, have a few beers and a bite to eat, then around 6 o'clock we will go to the house and leave loads of sticks outside with a note saying they're from the gardening centre for Jamie and we hope the whole family has a very lovely Christmas. Don't you think that will be a nice thing to do? Go and get him loads of sticks?'

'Go on then, I'm in,' says Juan wearily. 'Shall I come to the garden centre at 3 o'clock?'

'I'll see you then,' I say as I put the phone down and scan through the messages left on my phone.

There's a note from the Lebanese takeaway confirming lunch delivery for the grand date at the weekend, then about 20 requests for newspaper interviews from all over the world. Then there is one from Michael Foley, David Beckham's assistant. He tells me the trip has been organised, and we will leave on the 22nd and return on the 24th. 'See your emails,' he writes. 'All the details and tickets are in there.'

Oh brilliant! I forget about the interview requests from papers in China, Outer Mongolia and Luxemburg and rush to my emails. There it all is. All details of the cab will pick us up and take us to the airport, the hotel details and photos of Santa galore. There's a separate email for me to forward to Oliver's dad, Brian, so I do that, and go back to the email for me: there are pictures of reindeer on snowy plains, huskies, gorgeous food and pretty people in bobble hats. I need a bobble hat. Where can I get a bobble hat?

THE ARRIVAL OF JUAN

1 9TH DECEMBER

Juan and I cling onto one another as we stagger towards the small cottage, nestling in a quiet cul de sac off Cobham High Street. Oh, dear. I can't walk straight, and everything's just a little blurry. We drank way more than we'd meant in the pub, I'll be honest with you. We were only going for a couple, but there was such a lot of catching up to do, and then we were celebrating the whole Beckham thing and the trip to Lapland, so a couple of drinks turned into five or six and by the end of it all, well - not to put too fine a point on it - I feel very drunk.

We should have just staggered home to sleep it all off, but instead, we've found our way to this pretty cottage where the boy who wants sticks lives.

The two of us now stand in front of the beautifully decorated house, with the lovely giant wreath on the door and sparkly lights around the window frames. You can see the orange glow behind the heavy curtains, indicating that the lights are on inside. They're in. Now we need to provide them with sticks.

I notice that Juan is swaying a little. Or perhaps I'm swaying: it's hard to know. There is certainly a lot of swaying going on.

'OK, come on then,' I say to Juan. I can hear myself slur, and I notice how glassy his eyes look...you know, that look people have when they've drunk too much? Well, he has it—big time.

'Sshhhh...' he says, waving his finger in front of his face. 'We have to be quiet now.'

'Yes,' I whisper so quietly that he can barely hear me. 'Now we know where the house is, let's go into the park over there and collect the sticks, which we can leave on the doorstep. Yeah?'

Juan nods. I'm not sure he knows what I'm saying. He staggers along behind me as we try to walk towards the park. 'Have you got the letter with you for the little boy?'

'Of course,' I say, pulling the letter out of my pocket.

Dear Jamie,

Here are some sticks from Foster's gardening centre. I hope you enjoy playing with them.

I know you love sticks, so hopefully, these will be a Christmas treat. I hope you and your family have a lovely time over Christmas. Lots of love.

From,

Mary Brown and everyone working at Foster's DIY & gardening centre.

We start gathering as many sticks as we can carry, bundling them into black bags and tipping them onto the doorstep.

I'll be honest, it looks like we've just tipped out a whole heap of rubbish on their doorstep, but once they read the letter and remember the note that their son wrote, they'll be pleased that we took the time to do this.

I smile at Juan. What five-year-old wouldn't be delighted to come out of his house and see all this?' I say. 'I think we've made a kid very happy.'

'And you could make a 35-year-old very happy if you would accompany him back to Cobham High Street for another cheeky pint before we head home.

'Good thinking,' I say, as I see the curtain move slightly in the house as if someone is aware of our presence. 'Let's get out of here.'

The two of us power-walk (power stagger might be more accurate) away from the house, breaking into a mild jog as we hear a sound behind us. Then we go racing down the little country lane, which leads back to the centre of Cobham, laughing all the way. Finally, we emerge onto the High Street and give each other a high five before pausing to catch our breath.

'That was a cool thing to do.'

'It was. That kid will not believe it when his mum and dad show him all the sticks.'

'I know. It would be great to be there to see the boy's face when he realises the sticks are all for him.'

'You know you are covered in leaves and bits of broken branches, don't you? All over your jumper. Look at you...you're filthy' As Juan says this, he looks down and sees that his jumper is covered in bits.

'Oh Christ, I look like a vagrant,' he says, frantically brushing himself down before picking off the remaining debris bits and starting to help me.

'How have you got so much more than me on you?' he asks.

'There's a bigger expanse of jumper to attract leaves,' I reply, as he plucks bits off me like a cat grooming its kittens.

'Done,' he says, rubbing his hands together to remove the last vestiges of the rubble from his fingers.

'Come on then,' I say. 'It'll be last orders soon.' We start to move towards the pub door when a police car comes zooming towards us at top speed with its lights going, and its nee-naw, nee-naw, nee-naw blaring out.

'Someone's in trouble,' I say to Juan as it screeches to a stop next to us. 'Those boys don't look like they're messing around.'

We stand and watch for a minute as an officer jumps out of the car and runs towards us. I step aside to let them enter the pub, but the officer stops in front of me.

'Don't go in there,' he says.

'I'm not. I was opening it for you.'

'Come over to the police car,' says the officer. Juan lingers by the pub door. 'You too, sir.'

Another officer steps out of the car as we approach it, and the two of them stand in front of us., looking at us as if we're hardened criminals.

'We've had reports of two individuals hanging around in front of a house in Rose Avenue before dumping a load of gardening rubbish. The people described to us look very much like you.'

'Yes, it was us,' I say. 'Not loitering or anything. We weren't causing any trouble. We just dropped off a load of sticks.'

'You dumped a load of branches and mud on the doorstep.'

'Yes. Not mud - not really - we were mainly trying to put sticks there.'

'You dumped your gardening waste on their doorstep instead of taking it to a dump or disposing of it properly. That's fly-tipping. You also frightened the lady of the house by loitering outside in what she describes as 'a loud, drunken manner.'

'No, we didn't. No, you've got it all wrong,' I try. 'That's not what happened at all.'

'So, you didn't dump leaves, sticks and branches outside Mandarin Cottage on Rose Avenue around 20 minutes ago? Because I have descriptions here which match you...a fat, unkempt woman with messy hair and an effeminate-looking man who was jigging around constantly like he needed the toilet. Would you say that was an accurate description?'

'It's a bit harsh,' I said. 'My hair's OK, isn't it?'

'Did you or didn't you dump rubbish outside their house?'
'Yes, we did, but as a gift.'

'A gift.'

'They were sticks for Jamie, the little boy who lives there. Jamie wrote to me and asked whether he could have loads of sticks for Christmas, so we put them there as a present. We left a note with them.'

As I mention the note, it occurs to me that I don't recall leaving the note. I push my hand into my pockets and feel it in there; I pull it out and open it.

'Didn't you leave it with the sticks?' says Juan. It's the first time he's spoken since the police arrived. 'And - by the way - I wasn't jigging around like I needed the loo. I was just cold, that's all.'

I look up at the officer and show him my note. He begins reading it while I delve into my handbag and pull out the letter the kid sent us in the *Christmas Post Box of Wishes and Dreams*. I hand that over as well.

'The family didn't know why you'd dumped a load of sticks outside the property,' he says. 'It was a foolish thing to do even with the note. Could you not have spoken to the lady first?'

'Sorry,' I say, looking down at the floor as he speaks.

'Come with us,' he says. 'We'll go back to the cottage, and you can explain.'

Juan and I enter the police car, glancing at one another nervously.

'Will we have to put all those bloody sticks back?' Juan whispers. I shrug. I didn't know, but it seems likely.

We pull up outside the house, and the officer knocks on the cottage door - a miserable woman with short, badly dyed hair answers.

'That's them,' she shouts, pointing aggressively in my direction. 'They're the ones...'

The police officer steps forward and explains the misunderstanding. I stand there fiddling with my hair. Why did she describe it as messy? I don't have messy hair. Her hair is horrible. How dare she.

The lady looks at the letters. A little boy is sitting on the sofa.

'Jamie, come here and see what these people have brought for you,' she says, bending over to gather a handful of the sticks.' Jamie takes one look and lets out an almighty shriek: 'Sticks!' He gathers them into his arms, smiles at Juan and me and settles down to arrange them in what seems like size order.

'I'm sorry that we panicked,' says the lady. 'But I saw you were hanging around outside, and when I came out and saw all the mess, I was shocked. A police car was driving down the road, so I flagged the officers down.'

'It's OK; we were just trying to be Christmassy,' I say. 'I'm in charge of Christmas at the store. I decorated David Beckham's tree yesterday.'

Oh, God. The lady looks from me to the officers while her husband, sitting quietly on their brown sofa for the duration of the chat, coughs gently to himself as if passing a warning to her that if I think I decorated David Beckham's tree, I am clearly nuts.

'Why don't you stay for a drink,' says the woman.

'Sure,' I say. 'That's nice of you.'

'I was talking to the officers, actually, but you're welcome to stay too.'

Her husband coughs again to warn her about the dangers of allowing two raving nutters into the house. But the lady is not perturbed. Instead, she leaves the room to get us drinks, and her husband flicks on the television so he doesn't have to converse with us. Then she returns with a tray full of glasses. 'It's a little drop of brandy,' she says, handing out the drinks.

'Good heavens!' shouts her husband, forcing his poor wife to jump.

'What's the matter? It's only the cheap brandy, not the expensive stuff.'

'No, I mean - look - on the television.'

We all look past Julie and her tray of drinks to the television behind her, where I stand outside the Beckhams' house in all my festive glory. He turns the volume up, and they listen as I speak about how I decorated the Beckhams' Christmas tree.

They all look at me, awe-struck.

'I told you before that I decorated his tree. I went twice. That was filmed the first time.'

'What's her house like?' asks the lady while Jamie hugs his sticks, and her husband stares open-mouthed at the screen.

'Nice,' I say. 'A nice house.'

THE BLIND DATE GOES WRONG

*C*HAPTER 21 20TH DECEMBER
I look out the window to see a perfect winter's morning: crisp & fresh: the ideal day to meet the man of your dreams.

'Surprise, surprise,' I sing out in the semi-darkness as Ted stirs beside me.

'I'm Cilla Black,' I add, in case he didn't get the Cilla reference from the song.

'Good for you', he says, moving as if he's going to roll over and go back to sleep, but then he sits up and stares at me through sleepy eyes. His face is stubbly, his hair is all standing on end, and he scratches his chest hair like a baboon.

'Why are you, Cilla? Are you about to do something ridiculous, like take to the stage at the Royal Variety Performance, or develop a Liverpudlian accent?'

'No. I'm organising the blind date today... Like Cilla Black did. Do you remember her program 'Blind Date'?'

'Oh, I'd forgotten all about that. You've worked so much this week, do you have to work Saturday as well? Can they not just get on with the date without you? Do you have to be there?'

'I always have to be there when Christmas calls,' I say, standing on the bed as if preparing to give a Martin Luther King-type speech. 'Christmas doesn't confine itself to the days in the week; Christmas is everywhere. Christmas is all of us. When I am wanted for Christmas-related activities, I must go. And now I must leave...'

'Good God,' says Ted, pulling the duvet over his head and snuggling back down into it while I dance into the bathroom to prepare myself for the exciting day ahead.

Sitting on the bus to work, I think through everything I need to get done before this wonderful Christmas date. I've asked the guys from the warehouse to move the pagoda into the main area by the Christmas nativity scene and to have the beautiful Christmas trees, now decked out in the same decorations as the Beckham tree, lined up to create an alleyway of Christmas trees leading up to their lunch table. On the other side is the lovely Rick Astley team. I make a mental note to contact Astley's people and see whether he'll come and perform for us.

Then Mandy will run natural and artificial flowers through the pagoda. In the middle of it, all will be a table and chairs beautifully laid out with linen, crockery, and cutlery that we sell in the store. Keith is apprehensive about us damaging the things we use, but I've tried to tell him that this is a valuable PR opportunity. I can't lay the table with crockery from Marks and Spencer, can I?

There should be a lot of press interest; a lot of newspapers have been ringing the store to check the timings today. It's an excellent Christmassy story and a bit of fun. It's hard to see what could go wrong. If Belinda isn't interested in Daniel, or if Daniel isn't interested in Belinda, then they don't contact one another again, and they have had a free meal. Everyone's a winner.

By 12.30 pm, everything is ready in advance of our 1 pm sit down. I never expected it to look quite so fantastic. Ted and Juan have even come down to support me, and I've managed to persuade Juan to act as a waiter.

At five to one a rather handsome man approaches me. He must be in his late 30s and has a lovely rugged look, giving him a film star quality.

'Can I talk to someone about this date today?' he says, and I feel as if all my wishes have come true. He's bloody lovely. I smile at Belinda and see her go a deep shade of tomato.

This man is seriously yummy. She must be delighted.

'Of course,' I say to the man and hear Belinda giggling in the background. The familiar sound of Juan's voice saying, 'I would,' makes me smile. It's all going to be OK. The thing I was most worried about was what Daniel would be like. Now here he is. Ah. All panic over.

'Can you tell me what this date is about?' he asks. 'I've received information to be here at one o'clock. But I'm a little bit baffled. I'll be honest.'

'Please don't worry about a thing, Daniel,' I say as I guide him to the table and chairs laid out beautifully. 'You will have the most wonderful date with a beautiful woman. I signal for Belinda to come over, and she sashays across.

'Let me introduce you to your date for today. This is Belinda.' I stand back and open my arms to introduce the couple.'

'There's been some terrible mistake.' he says. 'I'm not Daniel. I'm Tom. The date isn't for me. The person who put the note into the box was my son.'

With that, a young boy walks out looking a bit shell-shocked, to be honest. 'How do you mean your son put the note in the box? I sent emails confirming everything and checking it was all OK,'

'Yes, and you sent them to him, but he's seven, so he doesn't know what a date is. He's seen it mentioned on some tv programme. I didn't know anything about it until this morning. He asked me to take him to the centre for his date with a lady.'

This is a bloody disaster. I look at Belinda, smiling to herself as she waits to join her man at the table. Except her 'man' isn't a man, he's a young boy.'

'But I asked his age,' I say.

'No, you didn't. He showed me all the emails this morning. You double-checked that he wasn't over 40, and he confirmed that he wasn't.'

Shit.

Daniel walks over and stands next to Belinda, who looks hellishly confused by the sudden arrival of a young boy. Meanwhile, the photographers start to take pictures.

'Are you single?' I ask Daniel's father.

'No, I am not; I'm married.'

'Are you happily married, though?' I try.

'Yes, thank you.'

'You wouldn't fancy a date with a lovely lady?'

'No, I most definitely wouldn't.'

Damn. OK. I need to act.

'Daniel, would you like a free Christmas tree? One just like David Beckham's?' I say to the boy. Daniel nods, so I move him away from the date area, signalling for his father to follow us. I lead them over to where the Christmas trees are sold and tell the guys there to give him any tree he wants. Then I shake hands with his father and apologise for the confusion.

Belinda is now looking very worried. Oh, God. The poor woman's got enough on her hands with her mum's dodgy boyfriend fancying her. The last thing she needs is to be romantically linked with a seven-year-old and then have it blasted all over the press.

'Are you OK?' asks Ted. 'You look worried.'

'Oh my God, you have to help me. I'm going to ask a massive favour.'

'Sure, go ahead,' he says. 'Ask me anything.'

'Will you please pretend you're the one who's on the date with Belinda and have lunch for the photographers?'

'What?'

'Pretend to be her date. Unfortunately, the real date turned out to be a seven-year-old, and I don't know what to do.'

'A seven-year-old?' says Belinda, joining the conversation.

'I'm sorry,' I say. 'I promise to make it up to you.'

'Come on,' says Ted, grabbing a rose from the pagoda, presenting it to her and walking her towards the table and chairs. 'Let's have a nice lunch, and we can both go and beat up Mary afterwards.'

'Sorry for all the confusion, ladies and gentlemen,' I announce as the two of them take their seats. 'I'd like to introduce you to Ted and Belinda, who are on the Christmas blind date today. They're available for any interviews or questions; then I think we should leave them alone to enjoy their date.'

There are a few questions that Ted battles through before the couple are allowed to sit and enjoy their food, a rather lovely spread from the local restaurant.

Once they are seated, and Juan is serving them, I back away from the scene, drop my head into my hands and wonder how I have managed to get this so bloody wrong. I should have rung the guy and checked him out properly, but all the distractions of Beckham and Lapland...I didn't do the work on this that I should have and I'm cross with myself. So now I'm forced to sit here hoping no one notices that my boyfriend is on a date with Belinda. When I think things can't get any worse, there's a tap on my shoulder.

'Excuse me, do I know you?' asks a familiar-looking man.

'I'm not sure. I work in the centre here. Perhaps you have seen me walking around?'

It's bound to be a David Beckham fan wanting to hear more about his idol, but I can't face any of that right now.

'No, I know where I saw you. You're the lady who walked up to our car last week and lay across the bonnet just as I was trying to leave the centre.'

'What?' says Keith. I hadn't realised he was standing right next to me.

'Oh, right. Yes. Ah, I'm glad you brought that up because that was a complete misunderstanding. I got you mixed up with someone else. Can you believe it? Many apologies.'

'It was strange. You just lay there pouting at me,' said the man, warming to his theme. 'I couldn't work out what was going on. But, really - it was the strangest situation, wasn't it, Emma?'

The woman with him nods. 'We thought you were dead at one point because you didn't move. Our son, Jacob, was terrified.'

'Yes, well - that's terrible. So sorry. Have you got everything you want in the centre today? Can anyone help you with anything?'

'No, we're fine,' says the man, and Keith looks at me quizzically while the two of them walk off.

'I hope you know what you're doing,' he says.

'Yes, of course, I do. The date is going well.'

'You think so? That's your boyfriend up there having lunch with her. I don't know what is happening.'

REMOTE-CONTROLS, CUKOO CLOCKS AND MADNESS

2 1st December
   'Where are you going now? I thought we might have a lie-in this morning before getting ourselves all packed for our trip to Lapland tomorrow,' says Ted.

'I won't be long. I'm just heading into the office to empty the *Post Box of*

Wishes and Dreams to see whether there's anything that needs actioning because I won't be able to do anything for the next few days while we're away, and then by the time we get back from our lovely trip, it will be Christmas Eve. So if there's something in there that needs dealing with, I should go and deal with it now.'

'OK,' says Ted. 'But everything you seem to 'deal with' from that bloody post box brings trouble. So be careful, OK? Don't get yourself arrested or beaten up trying to look after people, and particularly don't drag me into any more of your plans.'

'OK, I promise,' I say.

'And don't be long.'

'I'll be as quick as I can. I think Juan will come with me

and help me move some things around because Keith wants the Christmas trees to have a more prominent position in the shop for these final days before Christmas.'

'Juan can't move Christmas trees around; he can barely lift a bunch of flowers. So if there's heavy lifting to be done, I'd better come.'

Ted throws the duvet off and scratches his balls. He's a joy in the morning he is.

'There are guys in the shop who can move them. Honestly, there's no need to come unless you want to.'

I jump in the shower, get myself dressed in casual clothes and wander into the sitting room to see whether Juan is up yet.

He's sitting there on the sofa, painting his toenails a rather horrible shade of green...not a lovely emerald or soft turquoise, but a colour that makes him look like he's got gangrene.

'Why?' I say.

'I thought it would work well and look great with khaki trousers, but now I'm unsure.'

'No. Not great timing either - we're about to leave.'

Juan insists that it's OK: he'll wear flip-flops. It's freezing, but he doesn't seem put off by the idea of getting frostbite. And, anyway, don't toes that get frostbite to become gangrenous? He's short-circuited the whole thing by painting them the colour of gangrene in the first place.

'There's no point painting my nails if no one can see them, is there?' he says as he grabs flip-flops, shades and his man bag and sashays towards the door as if he's going to the beach.

We jump onto the bus and head for work. I'm pretty nervous about going in today after yesterday's fiasco, but I'm reasonably sure that Keith won't be there. By the time he sits me down and talks to me about it, I'll have been to Lapland

and got the best PR possible for the gardening centre, so he'll have nothing but praise.

As we walk past Big Terry, who's moving the Christmas trees away from where they were placed yesterday, flanking the romantic meal, to a prominent position in the centre, I'm excited about everything again. This place does look great.

There's a big sign saying:

Want your tree designed like Beckham's? Take a look at this and talk to the staff about how you can copy it at home.

The date may have been far from perfect yesterday, but we just about got away with it, and I'm sure the photos will look good and highlight the merchandise for sale in the store, and I did manage to decorate Beckham's tree, so it hasn't all been bad. And - of course - I'm taking the lovely Oliver to Lapland tomorrow. So it's been a Christmas to remember.

'Juan - do you mind just going over to the post box and taking out the letters in it,' I say, as I help put the decorations back onto the trees, they've moved them around so clumsily that half the Rick Astleys have tumbled off.

'If there are too many letters to carry, there's a carrier bag in my handbag.'

Juan goes to the post box while I reassemble the decorations.

'One bag enough?' I ask him as he returns.

'Err...yes,' he says. 'There's only one letter in there.'

'What? I thought there would be loads yesterday after the date. I expected it to be full to bursting.'

'Yeah, perhaps it will be next week?' he suggests.

'Next week is too late. The Post Box comes down on Christmas Eve.'

Juan hands me the solitary letter from a lady called Agnes, who is writing to the good people of Foster's garden centre to thank them for making it so Christmassy and lovely every year. She says it's a real treat for her to see how full of Christmas spirit the shop is. 'It's been the best place to go at Christmas,' she writes.

Ah, that's lovely. I feel genuinely pleased that we can bring such joy and happiness into the lives of our customers. I think it's an important thing to do. She says she has a present that she would like to give to the person responsible for making the store look so special. And she urges whoever it is to come to the house that evening to receive it.

'Oh God, I'm not going to any more customers' houses,' says Juan. 'Not on your life. Not after stick-gate. That was terrible. Let's keep right away from the customers' homes.'

'I don't know. I think it might be nice to pop round.'

'Have you forgotten that last time we did that, we ended up in the back of a police car? Just write a kind letter to them thanking them, but tell them we don't accept presents at Christmas.'

'You speak for yourself,' I tell Juan. 'I'm all about receiving presents at Christmas. So let's meet the customer, be nice to her, and graciously accept the present. After all, it's what she wants to do.'

'I guess,' says Juan. 'But you got to be a bit careful about these people. There are some right nutters out there. And I bet among the nuttiest are the people who contact the staff of the local gardening centre and invite them around for a 'present'.

'She lives about five minutes from my flat. Why don't we pop around there later? I'll feel better if we respond to as many letter writers as possible.'

'OK, it's your shout. But I'm not coming.'

'What do you mean you're not coming? You're my little partner in crime.'

'Yeah, exactly. That's why I'm not coming. See if Ted wants to go.'

'Oh yeah, Ted's going to want to come and knock on some woman's door.'

'He won't want to, and neither do I.'

At 7 pm that evening, Juan and I head towards the house belonging to the lady who put the letter into the post-box. He didn't take much convincing, as I knew he wouldn't. I think he secretly likes all the adventures I take him on.

He makes me lead the way, so I stride to the front door and knock gently. It says in the letter that her name is Agnes, but she likes to be called Mrs A.B. Walters. I hate to call people Mr or Mrs; it reminds me too much of school. But I don't want to upset her, so when she opens the door, I am reduced to calling her, Mrs Walters. I explain to her that I am in charge of Christmas at the gardening centre and I just wanted to thank her very much for her note, and how kind I thought it was of her to take the trouble to write in.

'Oh, do come in. I've got some cookies here. Have some cookies.'

'They could be poisoned. This house is weird,' says Juan, who is hiding behind me the whole time. From over my shoulder, I see him scanning the place like he's my security detail or something. We're invited to sit down and told to eat some cookies. Not offered them, but told to eat them. I nibble nervously on the edge of one while Juan's action-man eyes scan the place.

The thing is, the cookies are delicious. They are lovely. Any latent fears about my safety are swept away by the sweet taste of delicious, crumbly biscuit.

'This is for you,' says Mrs Walters, smiling in quite an odd way. She must be around 60, but she could be much younger. It's hard to tell. She's wearing an old-fashioned apron, and her house looks like it's from the 1960s, mainly brown and with very retro furniture. Quite awful.

I sit there, wondering what is 'for me' because she hasn't

handed me anything. Then she rushes out of the front room and into the kitchen, where I hear rustling paper.

Juan and I stare at the big old television while we wait. I notice there are cuckoo clocks everywhere. I mean *everywhere*. How bizarre is that? It's quarter to six, and I know we have to get out of the place before 6 pm because it'll be mayhem when they all start bursting out of their little wooden houses and cuckooing.

Mrs W is suddenly back in the room. She moves like a wild animal sneaking up on its prey, and she hands me a parcel wrapped so badly that it looks as if a pet terrier did it. I take it and smile.

'Thanks very much,' I say.

I am about to open it as her husband walks in through the door.

'Oh my my, we have visitors. Who do we have here then?' he asks. 'We weren't expecting visitors. You've given them my favourite biscuits as well.'

'My name is Mary, I work for Foster's gardening centre, and your wife sent a kind letter thanking us for how we decorated the garden centre at Christmas. I just came to wish her a Merry Christmas.'

I look at Mrs Walters; she's gone scarlet and is mouthing something to me behind her husband's back. When he goes into the porch to hang up his raincoat, she darts over to me and tells me to hide the present. 'Hide the present quickly. HIDE IT,' she shrieks. 'Don't let him see it.'

I push the present into my handbag. Juan glares at me as if to say - *we all knew this would happen. I told you, they're mad.*

When her husband comes back into the room, he looks at us as if he's surprised we're still there.

'Well, we must be off,' I say. 'Merry Christmas to you both.'

'Merry Christmas,' says Mrs M. 'From Malcolm and me.'

We walk outside, and she closes the door behind us.

'That was odd. Seriously, there is something wrong there. I don't know what, but something was weird. Do you think she's mental or something?'

'I don't know,' I say. 'She told us to come round, but her husband didn't want us there.'

'Perhaps it was a cry for help?' suggests Juan. 'Look at what the present is.'

I pull the bundle of scrunched-up paper out of my handbag and take the wrapping paper off. Inside is some sort of remote control.

'What on earth is that for?'

'I don't know. It doesn't look new. It looks like any normal household remote control,' says Juan, as he leans over and presses a few buttons to see what happens. As he presses, there's a loud shout from Malcolm on the sofa in the sitting room.

'Stop it,' he says.

I press another button, and he shouts again.

'It's a remote control to work, Malcolm,' says Juan. Through the window, we see Mrs Walters come in from the kitchen.

'Why does this TV keep going on and off?' he says.

'Oh fuck. It's their tv remote control,' says Juan, rather too loudly. Mr Walters looks through the window and spots us both standing there just as I press the button again, and the TV volume raises until it's bellowing out.

'Turn it down,' says Juan, but I can't remember which button I pressed, and we're in semi-darkness, so I can't see anything.

Malcolm comes out of his house and stands there with his arms folded. 'What on earth are you doing?' he shouts over the sound of people bellowing on his television. 'Why are you standing there with our remote control, pressing all

143

the different channels and moving the volume up and down?'

'I don't know,' I say because I can see his wife in the background, and she shakes her head viciously, indicating that she doesn't want us to talk to him.

'Is this your idea of fun?' he barks at Juan. 'You: the man with the flip flops and the green toes. Why are your toes green?'

'Oh, I painted them.'

'Did you steal our remote control so you could ruin my evening's television watching?'

'No,' says Juan, giving me a look of pure helplessness.

'Well, what are you doing with it then?'

Agatha is apoplectic now, jumping around behind him, begging us not to reveal that she gave it to us as a Christmas present.

'I don't know what's going on here. I have a good mind to call the police,' he says.

'Oh no. Not the police. Not again,' says Juan, which does nothing to make us look like the innocent party.

'I'm sorry. There's been a misunderstanding. Here's your remote control. I'm very sorry,' I say, handing it over.

He's about to bark something back at us when the neighbour pops her head out of her door and shouts to Malcolm to please turn the television down.

'I'm sorry, Emma,' he says. 'These two nutters from the garden centre stole our remote control.'

The lady comes out of her house and walks over to us. Bugger. I recognise her.

'I know you,' she says. 'You work at the gardening centre, and you threw yourself across my husband's car when we were driving away, and you lay there for about 10 minutes, refusing to move.'

'Right, I'm ringing the police,' says Malcolm, but his voice is drowned out by an almighty clatter as all of the cuckoo clocks burst into life and deliver their sounds. The noise is deafening, with the tv blaring out and cuckoo clocks singing.

'Time to go,' I say to Juan, and the two of us run like the wind.

MARTII THE VIKING & A
QUESTION FROM TED

*O*nce we are back at my flat, we race into the sitting
room and try to explain everything to Ted.

'And there were cookies, and the house was odd, then she
gave us their remote control, and the volume was too loud,
and the cuckoo clocks went off, and the neighbour turned
out to be this woman whose car I had laid on, so we ran, we
ran like the wind, but no police were called this time.'

'I don't understand any of that, Mary, but I'm happy the
police weren't called. Now, shouldn't you go and pack for
our trip to Lapland tomorrow? And have you filled in all
those forms they sent you, the ones asking for shoe sizes and
things?'

'Oh yes,' I say as I fill them in. I'd completely forgotten all
about them.

It takes me about 10 minutes to pack and about two
hours to find my passport; then I fall into bed. Being in
charge of Christmas has been quite hard. It's a lot of responsibility, you know. I don't know how Father Christmas
copes. No wonder he drinks so much.

· · ·

22ND DECEMBER

'Do you ever think to yourself, *how on earth did I get here?'*
asks Ted as the taxi driver pulls up outside Gatwick airport.

'No, never. I think it's perfectly natural to be on a trip to
Lapland with a one-legged boy to meet Father Christmas, all
organised by David Beckham.'

Ted laughs and takes the bags out of the boot. 'I don't
know how you manage it, Mary Brown, but I'm happy
you do.'

So, we're off. Brian and Oliver are travelling separately
because they're flying from Scotland, where Oliver has been
having treatment, and we'll meet up with them tomorrow
morning. For now, it's just Ted and me - off to a winter
wonderland of pink skies, reindeer sledges, frosty fir trees,
steaming hot chocolate and twinkling lights. And snow.
Snow everywhere. I've been looking at Lapland videos
online; it's a snow-filled fantasy. We are staying in the capital
- Rovaniemi - which is perched on the edge of the Arctic
Circle. Most importantly, it's the official home of Father
Christmas.

I plan to take loads of photographs and send postcards to
everyone I know.

When we arrive in Lapland, it's freezing cold. I realise
that shouldn't come as a surprise to me: of course, it's freezing. But I'm talking about a whole new level of cold here. So
cold that I'm wondering just how much wear I'm going to get
out of the strappy sandals that I insisted on bringing, even
though Ted said there was no point in bringing them because
I wouldn't get any wear out of them. Damn it. I hate it when
he's right.

I wrap my scarf around my neck, push my hands deep
into my pockets and look around me. I can't see a great
deal… it's dark and bitterly cold, even though it's only 3 pm. I
was hoping to take in all the wondrous sights while driving

along to Santa Claus Holiday Village, but despite peering out of the window like a small child, I can't see anything.

'You are here,' says the taxi driver. 'In the home of Father Christmas.'

'Thank you,' we both say as we clamber out of the warm car and move to collect our luggage from the boot.

'We will take care of that,' says a sizeable blonde man with a huge beard. He looks like a Viking. He's beautiful. He's an enormous, handsome Viking. Happy Days!

I see Ted standing up extra tall and puffing out his chest.

'I could look like that if I dyed my hair,' he says.

'Of course, you could, dear.' I don't add that he'd also need to grow a few inches and spend the rest of his life in the gym.

Viking man tells us that his name is Martii. 'You have come on the shortest day of the year, which makes it a special day,' he says. 'But also, quite a cold and dark day. We have ski suits here for you to wear, to keep you warm.' A lady steps forward with ski suits. She must be about 20, tall, blonde and fabulous.

'That's more like it,' says Ted.

'Maybe come in here to change?' she says, leading us into the hotel reception and a room just off the main lobby. I try on the ski suit hoping to God that it fits. I find it so embarrassing when things don't fit me. I filled in that form last night and said we both needed extra large sizes. Happily, the Laplandish extra-large is big, so for the first time in my life, I'm able to put on clothes which say they are extra-large and turn out to be extra-large. If anything, mine are a bit too big. And you won't find me saying that very often.

We walk back into the lobby, and Viking Man dazzles us with loads of interesting facts about the area, telling us that the line of the Arctic Circle runs right through the middle of the village. 'You can see it marked with a row of lanterns and blue lights,' he says in that lyrical, sing-song accent that makes me want to smile.

'Now I will take you on a reindeer sleigh ride so you can see some of it for yourselves.'

'Oh great,' I say, smiling warmly at Viking man. 'That would be lovely, thank you.'

'My very greatest pleasure.'

'I bet he takes steroids.' says Ted.

I jump onto Martii's sleigh (not a euphemism, sadly), and he takes us along the Forest Path, through fir trees piled up with snow as Ted and I snuggle up between blankets and reindeer hides. It's a wonderful, magical trip, and I want it to go on and on. We don't see anyone else in the snow as we skate along so gracefully that I feel like the sleigh might lift into the air and glide through the late afternoon sky. Some of the journey takes us through extensive forests of imposing trees; some skeletal, boughs hung with snow, others - fir trees, I think - dressed for the cold, displaying their pine needles like a peacock exposing its feathers.

Martii tells us to come back later that evening because water droplets will have crystallised on the branches creating magical Arctic art. He tells us that the ice looks like 'ladies' fingers.'

'You must see the sparkling icicles,' he says, making it all sound so poetic.

'And here is house,' says Martii, pointing to a small cottage which looks like something out of a fairy tale. There's an elaborate wreath on the door, and you can see the lights from the Christmas tree sparkling and welcoming through the windows.

'All your luggage is inside,' says Martii.

'Wow, thank you so much.'

Martii helps me off the sleigh and puts his hand out to help Ted.

'I'm OK, mate. Don't need any help, thanks,' says my boyfriend defensively.

'Tonight, you may come to see the northern lights with me after Lappish food is delivered to your door. OK?'

'Oh yes, I'd love that,' I say while Ted shrugs and says he's heard the northern lights aren't that special.

'Will you behave, Ted?' I say as we walk down the little path to our home for the next few days. 'Just because you don't like Viking man, doesn't mean you can spoil the whole trip.'

'Sorry, but he's a bit much. Chucking compliments around and driving a bloody reindeer sleigh.'

'You might need to get into the spirit of the thing a bit more,' I say. 'If you think he's too much, I don't know what you're going to make of grown men and women dressed as elves and Santa Claus tomorrow.'

'As long as they're not all 8' tall and with muscles bursting out of their shirts, I'll be OK. Let's go and unpack.'

We've put away all our clothes and adjusted to our tiny home when there's a gentle knock at the door, and an old man with a long white beard hands us a box of food.

'We have put extra pancake,' says the man. 'Any more food needed, call reception, and I'll be back.'

'Thank you very much. That's very kind,' says Ted.

Inside the box, there's a delicious soup with fresh salmon, a kind of pancake to go with the soup and some cookies with hot tea for dessert. We've just finished when there's another knock at the door.

'Blimey, we don't get this many visitors at home,' says Ted, trundling off to answer it.

It's Viking Man. He has arrived to take us to see the northern lights.

'We will go now to try to see the lights. I can make no guarantees about this, though,' Martii insists. 'It is a clear night, but you never know whether you will see them. We will go, but I cannot promise.'

'We understand,' I say, while Ted shrugs. He seems to go quiet and sulky whenever Martii is around.

'The Northern Lights are also known as Aurora Borealis,' Viking man continues, and they are pretty spectacularly beautiful. Very much like your girlfriend.'

I giggle like a schoolgirl at this. A handsome Viking who tells you you're spectacularly beautiful. What more could a girl want?

Ted drops his head into his hands.

It takes a while before we see anything. I mean, it feels like we drive, walk and wait for ages but then a faint grey-green stripe becomes visible in the sky.

'Watch it, watch it,' says Martii.

The stripe soon becomes a vivid shot of green; then, in no time, the sky looks like it's on fire, lit by green-purple flames. Green clouds of light begin to dance above us and smudge outwards, so they're all around us. I don't think I've ever seen anything quite so beautiful. It's entrancing; it makes you feel like you're being drawn into this magic artwork in the sky.

I stare up at it, mesmerised.

'Are you happy?' asks Ted, as we stand, wrapped around each other, watching the magnificent lights swirl around us.

'So happy. I'm the luckiest girl alive,' I say.

'No, I'm the lucky one,' says Ted. 'Look, there's something I want to ask you.'

'Sure.' I'm talking to Ted, but my eyes are fixed on the skies above us. When I eventually glance in his direction, he looks very serious.

'What is it? Is everything OK?'

'Mary - everything's perfect. I love you.'

'Oh, Ted. I love you too.'

'I'd like us to take things to the next step.'

'How do you mean?'

'I think we should move in together.'

'Really? Oh my God, I'd love that.'

'If we both get rid of our flats, we can buy a place that's our own.'

'Oh wow. Wow. Ted, I'd love that so much.'

'So would I,' he says. 'I can't think of anything better, to be honest. I want to be with you forever and ever.'

'Oh, me too, Ted. Me too.'

So here I am: standing in the snow with the northern lights dancing in the skies above me, as a large Viking claps and cheers at the news. I've thought a lot about Ted and I moving in together, but I never envisaged it being like this.

'Shall I take you back now,' says Martii. 'You have celebrating to do. Maybe you like to celebrate in bed?'

'Yes, it's getting late,' I say, ignoring his bed comment. The sky's colours fade away, but it's been incredible. The whole thing was surreal, as if great artists were floating through the sky, throwing paints around and drawing magnificent streaks of colour above us.

'This has been great,' I say to Martii. 'Thank you so much.'

'No problem. I enjoy showing you the lights. Now, I will enjoy seeing you in the morning. So enjoy your rumpy-pumpy celebrations.'

Oh, good God. These guys don't mince their words. Do they?

FATHER CHRISTMAS TIME

2 3rd December

'I'm so excited to meet Oliver,' I say to Ted when we wake up, all snuggled up in our cosy bed.

'It's a shame he's only coming for two days, though,' says Ted. 'I'd have thought they would have come early yesterday morning.'

'He's not well. His dad said that two days was the most he wanted to take him away for.'

'Yeah, I guess he can't be too far from his doctors. It must be tough. I do feel for him.'

'I know I can't imagine how it must feel. Can you picture having this lovely little boy who means the world to you but is in so much pain, and you can't do anything to help him.'

'I'm sure he looks after him well.'

'Yes, I'm sure he does, and I know Brian is at the hospital all the time with him and struggles to hold down his job because he needs to spend so much like with Oliver, but you can't take the pain away from him. That must be heart-breaking.'

'Where's Oliver's mum?'

'She died,' I say, trying not to cry, so Brian is dealing with this awful situation all alone. No mum to help share the worries and the joys. And how will he ever meet a partner if he can't leave Oliver alone? It must be so hard.'

'Come on now, Mary. Don't cry. We'll ensure he has the best time possible while he's here. Now, shall we get up?'

I nod because I'm scared to speak in case I start crying. Finally, Ted gets out of bed and shuffles off to the shower.

'We're meeting Oliver and Brian at 10 am at the main hotel so that they can get their ski suits.'

'So, how do we get there?' he shouts from the shower.

'I think Viking man is coming to pick us up and take us over there.'

'Oh, joy,' says Ted. 'Bloody wonderful…' Then his voice is drowned out by the water cascading down in the shower room.

By 9.30, Ted and I are showered, dressed in our padded ski suits, bobble hats and gloves at the ready, waiting by our cottage door. But it's not Viking man who turns up to take us out for the day; it's an older man. He looks like a Viking, too, to be honest, but nowhere near as big, hunky and handsome as yesterday's Nordic delight.

'I bet Martii didn't want to come,' says Ted. 'Now he knows we're going to move in together, and he's got no chance with you.'

'Oh, Ted. Honestly, you are so ridiculous. As if a man like that wants anything to do with me anyway.'

'He said you were spectacularly beautiful. And he's right. Then he said we were going to have rumpy-pumpy. He was right about that, too. But he shouldn't have said it.'

'He was being friendly. It's his job to make us feel good.'

'Well, he didn't make me feel very good when flirting with you.'

'Honestly, Ted, you are crackers sometimes.'

We head off to the hotel, and as soon as we arrive and I step off the snowmobile, I see Oliver. He looks just like his photo: incredibly pretty, with big blue eyes and this lovely pale blonde hair sticking out from beneath his furry hat.

'Hello, I'm Mary,' I say, stomping over to him in my big ski boots and waving like a lunatic. 'It's so lovely to meet you.'

His dad, Brian, has a captivating smile, like his son. He is handsome in a scruffy way - unshaven and tired-looking with his hair all over the place. But I guess he's got his work cut out with this little one, so, understandably, he's not groomed to within an inch of his life.

I give Oliver a big hug. And then wonder whether I should have done that. Is he unstable? Is he unsteady on his feet? He doesn't seem to be. He smiles and looks at me like he's not quite sure who I am. Brian shakes my hand and tells me he cannot begin to thank me enough for organising everything.

'Really, it's no problem,' I tell him.

'We saw lovely dogs, didn't we, dad?' says Oliver.

'We did, son,' replies Brian.

'We went on a husky ride when we arrived yesterday evening. It was all a bit terrifying. But good fun.'

'Oh my god, that sounds amazing. I'm so glad you got to do that. We had a reindeer ride, which was lovely, but probably not quite as adrenaline-surging as the Husky ride.'

'We went faster than the wind,' says Oliver, swinging his arms from side to side to show me the speed at which they travelled. And you know who we're going to meet now, don't you?'

'Well, I've heard a rumour, but I'm not sure whether it's true,' I say

'We're seeing Father Christmas,' whispers Oliver conspiratorially. 'In his Grotto, which is where he lives. Are you coming as well?'

'I am coming, and I'm looking forward to it. I hope you've been good, so you get lots of presents.'

'I'm always good,' says Oliver. 'The only time I'm not good is when I'm bad.'

We all laugh at this. Oliver is a lovely kid. I'm so glad I could do this for him. He seems to be having the time of his life.

We climb onto the snowmobile that is taking us over to Santa's Grotto, and I sit next to Oliver while Ted and Brian take the seats behind us. Oliver is charming company. He even tells me about his leg and how he only has one and has to wear a 'falsie'.

'I'll show you later if you like, but I can't show you now because it's in my ski suit tucked into my boot, and I can't get to it.'

'That's okay. I think you should keep your ski suit tucked in to keep you nice and warm.'

'You've got to keep nice and warm when it's snowing and cold like this, haven't you?'

'Oh, you have,' I confirm. 'I nearly forgot to bring my hat. My head would have been icy, wouldn't it?'

Oliver laughs and tells me he would have lent me his hat if I'd forgotten mine. I give him a warm hug before we fall into a relatively peaceful, comfortable silence, looking out at the colossal fir trees painted thickly with snow. Before long, we start to see the signs telling us we're approaching Santa's grotto. I hear Ted and Brian chatting companionably behind us as we zoom along. Lovely Ted is asking him how he copes and how difficult it must be to do this alone.

I hear Brian telling him that it's hard but worth it. He says he'd love to meet someone and have a relationship, but he doesn't see how it would be possible.

'I'd have to meet an exceptional woman who would be kind and thoughtful enough to give me the space to spend time with Oliver when I need to. I don't think it will happen while Ollie is so young.'

I hear the words without thinking, but then a thought bursts into my mind.

And you know what that thought is: Belinda. How great would that be?

Belinda is kind and thoughtful and would be perfect for Brian.

Quite how I'm going to bring this subject up with him, and ask him whether I can make an introduction, is something I can't quite get my head around at the moment, but bring it up I must because this, Ladies and Gentlemen, might be the kindest thing I could do for this man and his lovely son.

We arrive at Santa's grotto and are greeted by elves who put down the toys they are making in the toy factory and wave at us like long-lost friends before they rush to help us off the sleigh.

If they're surprised to discover only one child on the sleigh carrying four people, they manage to hide it and treat us all to a charming welcome. The scene is beautiful as we watch dancers, singers, and elves frolicking in the snow. This is a wonderful place for children, but it feels odd for Ted and me to go in and meet Santa.

'I think I might be too big to sit on Santa's lap,' I say.

'And I'm too big,' says Ted.

'I'm not too big,' says Oliver quickly.

'No, you're the perfect size. Why don't we let you go in to see him, and we'll wait outside and see you afterwards.'

'OK,' says Oliver. 'I will show you all of my toys when I come out.'

'Yes, please. I'm looking forward to seeing them,' I say.

Once the two of them have trundled off, Ted turns to me: 'Fancy some of that gluhwein over there?'

There's a stall on the far side, dishing out a rather pungent-smelling hot alcoholic drink. It feels like the best thing we could do for ourselves at 11 am, so we stroll over, sit on the bench and sip away. It's idyllic, snuggled up to Ted, being warmed by love and alcohol. We only have a couple each, but I soon feel quite drunk; in that hazy, nothing matters; life is wonderful sort of way.

'I sometimes forget how lucky I am, but right now, at this moment, I'm aware of how great my life is,' I tell Ted. He looks a little shocked at my serious tone, so I suggest he gets us some more gluhwein.

Three glasses are too much. I feel very wobbly. I know I'm smiling like an idiot and wobbling my head around because I always do that when I'm drunk, and I can see Ted smiling at me in his lovely, indulgent way.

It feels like we've only been there a short while when I hear a shout in the distance.

'Look, look…'

We both spin around.

'Look at these! I've got presents,' squeals Oliver. He is hugging the biggest teddy bear I've ever seen. His father carries a separate box with a train set in it - something that Oliver has always wanted.

'I'm so excited,' says Oliver. 'I can't wait to show my friends.'

'We're going down to the children's party now. Do you want to come?' asks Brian.

'Yeahhh…party!' I shout, staggering to my feet, but Ted guides me back into a seating position.

'I think we'll give the party a miss and go and get something to eat,' says Ted.

'I don't blame you,' says Brian, being led away by Oliver. 'Hopefully we'll see you later.'

DAVID BECKHAM & RICK ASTLEY

2 4th December

The following day, I have a terrible hangover.

'Why do I feel as if my life is coming to an end?' I ask Ted.

'I have no idea,' he responds. 'I don't suppose it would be the three glasses of gluhwein followed by wine followed by more gluhwein late last night.'

'Really?'

'Yep. You were a disgrace.'

'I'm so sorry we didn't have dinner with Brian and Oliver last night. Did we let them know that we wouldn't be joining them?'

''You mean you're sorry that you didn't have dinner with them? I went.'

'You what?'

'I met them for dinner, and very nice it was.'

'Where was I?'

'Crashed out, face down on the duvet, dribbling.'

'Nice. Well, as long as I wasn't embarrassing or anything.'

. . .

WE FLY BACK to the UK later that afternoon. Oliver clutches his bear, and I clutch onto Ted. As long as I manage not to be sick on the flight, everything will be OK. When we land, I have one last surprise for Oliver: David Beckham will be at the airport to meet him. We've already established that he's a big David Beckham fan, so I'm hoping he'll be thrilled by the surprise.

Ted takes Oliver for a walk at the airport while I sit quietly with Brian. I'm unsure how to address this, but I'm determined to see whether he'd be responsive to a romantic introduction. 'Look', I say eventually. 'I'm sorry this is a bit embarrassing, but I've got this lovely friend who's single and dying to meet someone. Do you mind if I give her your number? You know, put the two of you in touch?'

'Gosh. Really? I'm not sure anyone would want to take on someone like me.'

'I think Belinda would love to take on someone like you. You're kind, fun and an incredible dad.'

'That's very kind of you,' he says. 'Tell me a bit about her.'

I put her name into Google to call up her picture on the company website. 'I can show you what she looks like,' I say, waiting for a picture to download. But the image is not of her at work, but of her on the fake date that went wrong.

'Oh, is that her? What does that say? *A magnificent date for two locals*. But isn't that Ted?'

'Yes, it's a rather long story. I won't bore you with the details, but - yes - that's her having lunch with my boyfriend.'

Brian looks unsure.

'Why would she be on a romantic date with Ted?'

'Don't worry about that - all a big misunderstanding. Just focus on the lady sitting there. Belinda is a sweet, lovely person. I think you'd like her a lot.'

'Okay. I'll give it a go,' says Brian, handing me my phone

back. 'But please make sure that she's aware of my family situation. I'm not the easiest person to date.'

'Brilliant,' I say as we board the plane and prepare to head home for Christmas. 'I'll fix something up once we're back.'

I sit next to Ted on the flight home, and we spend much time discussing what sort of home we want.

'I want somewhere cottagey,' I say. 'You know - the whole roaring fire, little garden, pretty cottage thing. Let's look at some more houses when we get back. We could even go out and go round seeing what's on the market.'

'Not tonight,' says Ted as the pilot announces that we're coming into land. 'I want you to do me a favour…don't make any plans for tonight. We've had a madly busy week, and we're visiting family tomorrow. It's Christmas Eve, and I'd like the two of us to be home together for once. Alone. OK?'

'Of course,' I say. 'That would be lovely.'

We arrive at Gatwick airport, and the four of us are taken aside and told there is someone to meet us. 'He's someone who really wants to meet Oliver,' says the airport official.

Oliver looks intrigued and Brian looks a little concerned; then, out walks David Beckham, causing Oliver to squeal like a puppy. Next, Ted squeals, and then Brian. I say, 'Hi David, how lovely to see you again', and - I swear to God - I feel like the coolest person ever to walk the earth.

David chats to Oliver and gives him piles of presents, including signed football shirts and tracksuits and some amazing computer games. I stand on the edge of it all, watching with pride and staring at David's bottom in what could be described as an inappropriate fashion.

As Oliver and David talk, my phone rings. I answer the call and hear Keith's dulcet tones on the other end. I assume he's calling to find out how the trip went, but he sounds like he's in a disco.

'Where on earth are you?' I say.

'I'm at work. Rick Astley's just turned up, and he's entertaining the crowds.'

'What?'

'Yes - he saw the Rick Astley decorations on the Christmas trees when the blind date feature was in the paper, and he came down to meet you. Hurry back.'

I look over at Ted, sitting there on his own, patiently waiting for me.

'Actually, I won't be back at the centre tonight. I'm going to head home now, but have a lovely Christmas, and please thank Rick for me, and get lots of pictures of him in front of the Rick Astley decorated tree, OK?'

'Are you serious?' says Keith. 'This is Rick Astley. He's about to sing '*Never Gonna Give You Up*'.'

'It sounds great, Keith. Have a lovely evening. I'll see you next year.'

I smile at Ted. 'Let's go,' I say. 'We've got a whole, wonderful future to plan.'

HOME SWEET HOME

I'm going to be completely honest with you; the minute I put down the phone, I feel a wave of disappointment. I really like Rick Astley, and - obviously - *Never Gonna Give You Up* is my favourite Rick Astley song because it's the only one I know. Perhaps we should head down there and watch him perform after all.

'Ted, if you want to go to the centre to watch Rick Astley, just say, OK. I've told Keith that we won't be there, but I don't mind going if you really want to.'

'Nope. I've no interest in going anywhere near your work today,' saysTed. 'I'm excited about spending the evening with you and waking up tomorrow morning and going to mum and dad's.'

Yeah. Christ. This is where it gets complicated because – as you know – I still haven't told him that we are committed to spending Christmas with both sets of parents. I genuinely believe he should tell his mum that we can no longer go there; I can't possibly tell mine after the disaster of me announcing on This Morning that my mum was a drug pusher. She really will take it personally if I now announce

164

that I'm not coming for Christmas or that Ted can't make Christmas.

The only alternative I can think of is to go to both sets of parents and have lunch with them all. Ted won't be all that delighted; I know he'd like to go to his parent's house properly. But I can't think how else we can handle this without offending.

Later that night, I'm at home with Ted, curled up on the sofa, having wrapped all the presents and feeling wonderful. Ted's watching the news while I laze rather sleepily, sipping my wine.

'You know what I think,' he says. 'I think I wouldn't have a square if I were a dictator.'

'What? A square?'

'Yes - like Red Square and Tiananmen Square...all the problems, uprisings and murders...they always happen in squares. You shouldn't have one. There you go - that's my tip for dictators.'

'Very good,' I say, drifting off to sleep. 'If I become a dictator, I'll bear that in mind. Oh - and - by the way - I've cocked up.'

'In what way?' asks Ted innocently.

'I have promised my mum that we will go for Christmas lunch with her tomorrow.'

'Whaaaat? Are you serious?' he asks. 'You've told your mum we'll be there when you know that I've told my mum that we'll be at hers.'

'Yep.'

'That's a disaster. I can't cancel, mum. She's been shopping and has bought everything already, and she did ask first.'

'Well, no, technically, I don't think she did. Mine did...and I said 'yes,' but when I arrived at yours, you were so excited about going to your mum's that I couldn't face telling you.'

'What are we going to do?' he says. 'I don't want us to

spend Christmas apart. And I thought your dad didn't like meeting new people.'

'He doesn't, and he hates having anyone in the house. All he wants to do is watch programmes about Margaret Thatcher. Amazingly, he's said you can come over. I can't cancel. But - I have a plan.'

'Go on.'

'Well,' I say. 'My mum's lunch is at 1 pm, and yours is at 4 pm.'

'Two lunches?'

'Unless you can think of a better plan.'

'Is there ever a better plan than two lunches?'

CHRISTMAS MORNING

2 5th December

I wake up most mornings and think, 'when can I eat?' I open my eyes and scan the room, and perhaps kiss Ted good morning, but all I can think about is when I'm going to get something to eat. When will I taste hot buttered toast with lashings of peanut butter on top? Thick bread, thick butter, thick peanut butter...big bite. God, I can feel myself salivating at the thought of it.

Food is my overriding concern all the time. If I feel happy, I want to celebrate with food; if I feel sad, I want to fall into food and fill myself with it until I can't feel the pain anymore. The thing I want to do more than anything, all the time, is eat. On 364 days of the year, I am trying to moderate myself and control myself around food. I wake up every day determined to pace myself and not eat all the day's calories before 8 am. I try to leave meals as late as possible, so I don't have time to overeat.

But Christmas Day is the one day of the year when I don't have to do any of that because the day is free of the usual food timing restraints. You can eat what you like when you want - it's the law. No one can tell you off for having three sherbet dib-dabs and five jelly babies or having a bowl of custard before breakfast. It's all allowed. No one will tell you that you are going to spoil your lunch. Nutty food combinations in unspeakable quantities are positively encouraged; you can delight in it... If you say, 'I'll have a plain boiled egg,' people will laugh, 'no, you won't - you'll have Baileys flavoured popcorn, and pop tarts dipped in marmite - it's Christmas. What's wrong with you?'

In some ways, you'd think this would be a living nightmare for someone like me with a food addiction, but it's not. It's really not. Once all the rules disappear, and I cannot beat myself up for breaking them, I feel much happier and more comfortable with myself. If I have honey ice cream and chips for breakfast, that's fine. On any other day, if I had honey ice cream and chips I would hate myself for it, and feel weighed down with guilt and disgust with myself, and it is those feelings of disgust that will push me headlong into food and cause me problems for days after my one bit of naughty behaviour occurred. It's the disgust that does for me; that's what causes me problems.

But not at Christmas. Oh no. It's 7.30 am on Christmas morning and I've eaten an entire box of After Eights. I mean - how rebellious is that? It's not even after eight in the morning, let alone after eight in the evening, and all that is left of the previously full box are scattered wrappers and the pungent aroma of fresh mint. I wander into the kitchen and see the bottle of ginger wine on the side. 'Oooo…' I think, but - no - even I have some standards. Gurgling ginger wine at the crack of dawn is the route to insanity.

'What are you doing up and wandering around instead of being tucked up in bed next to me?' says Ted, walking into my tiny kitchen behind me and wrapping his hands around my waist.

'Mmmm...you smell nice,' he says. 'What is that? Have you just cleaned your teeth?

'It's After Eights,' I reply proudly. See - no shame, no embarrassment, no disgust, no lying to hide my ridiculous eating habits - I tell Ted quietly and confidently and he doesn't bat an eyelid. 'Excellent start to the day,' he says. 'That ginger wine looks nice.'

'I thought that, but that's a bad idea. We'll be fast asleep by 10 am if we get started on that, and we've got two lunches to go to today.'

'OK, well, why don't I just give you this instead,' he says, handing me an envelope. 'It's a book token...I didn't know what else to get you.'

I try to hide the feeling of disappointment welling up inside me. A book token?

'How nice,' I say, gingerly opening the envelope. I don't want any bloody books. I wonder whether I can swap it for cash. Is that ungrateful?

I pull out the paper inside, but it doesn't say anything about books. It's a ticket to Greece for the holiday of a life-time. I look at Ted open-mouthed...a holiday? Not books?

'Of course, it's not books,' he says. 'I thought it would be nice if we went away on holiday.'

'Oh my God, oh my God, oh my God. Best. Present. Ever,' I squeal. 'This is just amazing.'

I feel bad now that I only got him a jumper and some boxer shorts.

11.30 AM:

Santa hat? Check.

A massive pile of presents? Check.

A bottle of really strange, green alcohol that I won in a tombola and think mum might like? Check

'Come on then, let's go,' I say to Ted, knowing that by now, mum will be peering out of the window, desperate for us to arrive.

'Coming,' says Ted, walking through the flat with a small bundle of presents.

'What are they for?'

'Well - I might have an extra one or two for you, and I've got presents for your mum and dad - nothing much, just little thank-you gifts for inviting me to join them for lunch.'

Bugger.

I have no extra presents for Ted, and it never even occurred to me to bring gifts for his parents. I'm bloody useless! And I'm Mary Christmas...I'm supposed to be in charge of Christmas.

'Hang on. Hang on,' I say.

I have presents under the bed. I've just remembered.

'Be back in a sec,' I say to Ted, tearing past him and reaching under the mattress, past the dozens of shoes that I never wear because they are too tight or too high (but they look lovely, so I'm not throwing them away).

There!

Nestling between some candyfloss pink wedges and a pair of way-too-small gold sparkly trainers that no one over four should wear, are three little presents. I can't even remember what's in them...they've been here since last Christmas. It's probably chocolates or a book or some other generic present. Enough to make it look like I've made an effort without looking like I've gone over the top. I pull them out, drop them into a carrier bag and rush out to join Ted.

'Let's go!' I say.

We squeeze into Ted's car and head off. Neither of us can get the seat belts around us, but we do our customary thing of trying to do it, then shrugging at one another in despair.

I'm looking forward to the day I can get it around me; it will feel like a tremendous achievement.

Ted heads off with us both sitting there, wilfully breaking the law as we ease through Cobham streets, heading for mum's house in Esher. Ted's quiet on the journey; I can tell he's feeling nervous. He hasn't met my mum and dad before, and I imagine that meeting them for the first time on Christmas Day must make it feel all the more daunting.

'Just here on the left,' I say as Ted swings the car into a small space. I look up and can see the curtains flicker a little. I knew it.

Mum's been looking out of the window all morning, waiting for us to arrive. I dread telling her that we have to leave at 3.30 pm (we're going to Ted's mum's for Christmas lunch at 4 pm, but I'm not telling my mum that, so please don't mention it).

'I bet they won't like me,' says Ted sulkily. 'They'll probably think you can do much better than me...and they'd be right. You're so lovely; you could have anyone.'

'Stop it, Ted. That's not true; I couldn't have anyone else. I'm desperate. That's why I'm with you.'

'Oh great, thanks very much.'

'I'm joking, Ted. For goodness sake. You know I'm joking; I love you; I think the world of you.'

Ted hugs me. 'Sorry for being sensitive, but it matters to me that I make a good impression on your mum and dad.'

'I know. And I love you even more for that,' I say. 'Don't expect too much communication from my dad. He's a bit of a nightmare.'

'Mine too,' says Ted. 'Mine too.'

Mum answers the door and throws her arms around me, hugging me closely. 'Happy Christmas, darling girl,' she says, grinning from ear to ear. 'A very merry Christmas.'

'This is Ted,' I say, indicating him, standing nervously by my side, clutching the mountain of presents.

'Hello, lovely to meet you,' says mum. 'Please come in.'

Ted follows me into our hallway, where the smells of Christmas lunch hang alluringly in the air.

'Smells delicious,' he says, and mum smiles warmly. 'Thank you.'

It's not all quite so cordial when we meet my dad. He looks Ted up and down and says: 'Blimey, Mary. You managed to find a bloke who's fatter than you.'

'Indeed,' says Ted, apparently unfazed by dad's rudeness. 'Nice to meet you, sir.'

He then turns to my mum and asks: 'Is there anything I can do to help?'

'Honestly, no - it's fine. Everything is under control,' says mum.

'I'm quite handy with a carving knife,' he says. 'So - please say if I can do anything.'

'Of course,' says mum demurely. 'Thank you, Ted.'

And I swear, in that minute, I fall more hopelessly in love with Ted than I've ever fallen in love with anyone before. I think mum does, too. She kind of swoons and has to hold on to steady herself. Well, it's either a swoon, or she's been at the wine already; hard to tell for sure.

'Ted, please, take a seat,' she says, indicating the furniture in front of us. Dad is in his favourite armchair, scowling at us; there is the small two-seater sofa and the other armchair - old and rundown but madly comfy. Ted wisely chooses the armchair. He sits down heavily and smiles at my mum.

'A little Christmas drink?'

'Please,' he says.

'Ooooo...look what I've got,' I interject, handing her the bottle of bright green liquid that I'd brought with me.

'Great,' she says, unconvinced by the lurid colour of the

drink. But mum's unfailingly polite and wouldn't want to dismiss the gift, so minutes later, she reappears with several glasses of the stuff to hand out. Oh dear, this wasn't the plan. The last thing I wanted was to drink it; I hoped to get rid of it here so mum would have it sitting in her kitchen rather than mine.

'Well,' says mum, blinking furiously after taking a swig. 'Is this what the young people are drinking these days?'

'I thought it might be nice to try something new,' I say, taking a swig and stepping backwards in alarm. It sure has a hell of a bite; I feel like a tiger has gnawed my throat.

'I'll get a bit more, shall I?' says mum, and I know, in that very moment, that we are all going to get hammered. The chances of Christmas lunch arriving at anything close to the suggested time or in anything like an edible state are becoming increasingly remote.

But it's Christmas, so we don't worry about those things. Mum comes back into the room, and we get stuck in.

'I'd love some more, please,' I say. Meanwhile, Ted has yet to take a gulp. Everyone is looking at him as he lifts his glass to his mouth and pours some of the acidic solution down his throat.

'No,' he squeals, choking and lifting his legs in some involuntary action to the impact of the liquid. Unfortunately, though, mums old armchair isn't used to quick, unpredictable, violent movements from 25 stone men, and his legs go up just as the backseat goes down behind him. Suddenly he's upside down in a broken armchair, trapped and struggling to get back onto his feet.

'Oh my goodness,' says mum as she and I rush over to try and help him up. Ted looks mortified as he struggles to get his (massive) arse out of the chair and get himself upright. The more effort Mum and I make to assist him, the worse we seem to be making it, so much so that we are forced to admit defeat and step back and watch him struggle and squirm as he scrambles to his feet.

'Well, that didn't go well,' he says, finally. He's got sticky green liquid all down his shirt, and the remains of mum's favourite armchair lie on the floor. 'This isn't the impact I hoped to have,' he adds. 'I'm very sorry.'

But mum and I are too busy laughing to hear his apologies. The impact of the strong alcohol, combined with seeing Ted jammed upside down with legs and arms in the air, has left us crying with joy. 'I don't think I've ever seen anything so funny in my life,' I say.

Mum tries to speak, but laughter gags her, and she splutters and smiles, and when she realises she can't talk at all for laughing, she leaves the room and runs into the kitchen to get more of the terrible drink I bought.

'This is going so terribly badly,' mutters Ted. Dad is sitting there watching the scene unfold, mum's laughter can be heard from the kitchen, and I'm rather uselessly dabbing at Ted's once-white shirt with a tissue I've found on the side.

'I'm very sorry,' says Ted to dad. 'I'm such a bloody clumsy fool.'

Ted looks heartbroken. It's clear he hoped to make a good impression on my parents, and he feels he's completely blown it. 'I'm sure you're probably thinking ', who is this big, fat, useless fool'...I'm not usually so unbelievably careless,' Ted is saying.

Perhaps it's Ted's contrition that gets to my dad, maybe it's the taste of the indescribably bad alcohol, or perhaps it's just the festive spirit, but he does what he's never done before - he smiles, then he laughs, then he says to Ted. 'Well, son, you've certainly broken the ice.'

It's bizarre and unpredictable, but the broken armchair situation has lifted this family Christmas, with mum and dad smiling and laughing while Ted apologises profusely for the mess of an armchair by his side.

Next, it's time to give Christmas presents, and we have this bizarre tradition in our house where my mum gives my dad the same Christmas card every year, and he doesn't remember from year to year. It's always been a joke between mum and me. Dad looks at it, smiles, thanks her for it and puts it on the mantelpiece, oblivious to the fact that he's been given the same card for the past 30 years.

Mum hands the card over to dad and winks at me. Dad opens it (mum invests in a new envelope every year, but that's it). He surveys the dog, reads the message and puts it on the mantelpiece.

'Ted,' he says. 'You see that card?'

'Yes,' says my boyfriend.

'Well, that dog is about 30 years old but hasn't aged a day.'

'How do you mean?' asks Ted. I haven't told him about mum's dog card tradition.

'My wife has given me the same bloody card every year since we married, and she doesn't think I've noticed.'

'Ohhhh,' mum and I both cry. How the hell has he noticed something like that?

'God, dad. We rely on you to be unobservant at all times. It's heartbreaking that you've started noticing things.'

'I notice lots of things,' says dad. 'I've noticed the bloody card coming every year, but I'm too polite to comment. But now you've brought Ted along, and he's started smashing up the furniture; I guess it might be time to speak up.'

'Well, I'm very disappointed,' I say.

'Me too,' says mum. 'I'm going to have to go out and buy a new bloody card now.'

Mum refills our glasses, and we all comment that the sickly sweet, green liquid is rather palatable after a couple of glasses.

'The more you drink, the better it gets,' says mum with a little 'hick'.

'So, tell me about Mary when she was younger,' says Ted.

Mum, Ted and I are sitting in a row on the small sofa without any other seating. The whole thing creaked when we all sat down on it, and I'm hoping it doesn't break. That would be too mortifying for words. The truth is that the sofa is built for two small people - not two enormous ones and one average-sized person.

'Well, there was this one time when Mary went abroad. We don't go in much for abroad in this house, so it was quite an occasion,' says mum, and I know straight away what bloody story she's going to tell...it's her favourite one.

'Mary was going to fly with 'assisted travel' which means someone would look after her on the flight. Now, the way they do this is to clip a tag on the child's coat and give you a code, and you can go online and track your child's journey...see where they are at any time. It's a good system.'

'Yes, that sounds like a perfect system,' agrees Ted.

'But, do you know what our Mary did?'

'No,' says Ted, looking over at me.

'As a joke, she took the clip off her blouse and clipped it onto someone else's bag. That meant that when I went to the site to check where she was, it brought up a map of the world, and I could see her plane taking off, veering the wrong way, and then flying off to Spain. I was beside myself! I had to ring up the company, screaming and saying my little girl was on the wrong flight. It wasn't perfect. Awful.'

'You little horror,' says Ted, shaking his head at me. 'How could you do that to your poor mum? Perhaps I can make it up to you with these presents.'

Ted pulls out gifts for mum and dad. He hands over the one for mum first, and she can't hide her delight.

'How amazing. Thank you so much,' she says, turning a

deep shade of pink. She tears off the wrapping to reveal a lovely silk scarf. It's very beautiful, with peacock blue and navy swirls through it.

Mum is thrilled. 'Thanks so much,' she says, wrapping it around her neck. 'That's very kind of you.'

Next, he hands a package to dad. I'm astonished at his bravery. I struggle to work out what to buy, dad. I've no idea how Ted has managed to think of something.

Dad tears off the paper to reveal a book about Margaret Thatcher...he almost drops it in surprise.

'This is great, thanks, Ted,' he says. 'She'd a fascinating woman. I will enjoy reading this. Thanks, son.'

'Lunch is ready,' says mum, as Ted and I snuggle up a little closer on the sofa. 'All come to the table.'

We all sit down and survey the mammoth amount of food before us. Mum has no idea this is the first of our Christmas lunches, so she's pulled out all the stops.

'What will your parents be doing for Christmas lunch?' she asks as if she's reading my mind.

'They'll just have lunch together,' says Ted. 'Just mum and dad.'

'Were they sad that you wouldn't be with them this year?'

'Yes, a little, but they are glad I'm spending Christmas with Mary.'

'How nice,' says mum. 'Turkey?'

We are going to have to leave straight after the Queen's speech to get to Ted's on time, but as the time rolls around and we're all seated on the tiny sofa waiting for it to start, I have a sudden emotional pang, I don't want to leave mum and dad's house. I don't want to go galloping across to Ted's mum and dad's house when Ted's dad can be so funny with me while mine is behaving with such extraordinary friendliness. It feels so cosy sitting next to one another. The absence of an armchair is working out just fine, though it does look like we're waiting for a bus or something. I wish Ted's parents could come instead of us going there, but I know his mum's been cooking dinner all morning. We must make an effort.

The queen's face looms on the screen, and we all lean forward.

'Do you remember when you thought Prince Philip had a huge bottom,' says my dad, laughing away to himself.

'What's this?' asks Ted.

'Mary heard them say 'three cheers for Prince Philip' and thought they said, 'three chairs for Prince Philip'. She thought he must have a massive bottom.'

Thanks, Dad.

CHRISTMAS AT TED'S

J walk into Ted's front room and see that they have
had a change around in the furniture. They have a
new TV, and - Christ alive - it might be the most giant TV
I've ever seen. Most of the living room is plasma.

On the one hand, I feel like congratulating them on
having enough money to buy such an enormous television;
on the other hand, I'm tempted to criticise them for not
having enough money to buy a house big enough to go
around it…

We exchange hugs and warm greetings of the season, and
I sit on the sofa.

'Here are some nibbles; you must be starving with us
having lunch so late,' says Ted's mum, handing me a plate
with mini sausage rolls, mini chicken satays and other
delights. 'And take this too,' she adds, passing me an enormous mixing bowl full of crisps.

'Yum,' I say. 'Yes – starving.'

Ted looks at me like I've gone insane, but I'm not sure
what else to do. I don't want to tell her we've already had one
Christmas lunch. I'm sure she'd be offended.

'Shall we play a game before we eat,' says Ted's mum, full of enthusiasm. Ted and I think this is an excellent idea because we've drunk about four pints of green alcohol, but Ted's dad is less convinced. He grunts.

'It'll be fun,' she insists.

'No, it won't,' he says.

I glance at Ted, and he raises his eyebrows. Ted's dad makes my parents look positively friendly. I feel sorry for Ted's mum; she's trying so hard. Ted's dad sits there and doesn't engage us. It's all down to her to make the day work.

'I'm not playing any bloody games. Let's eat.'

'Sure,' Ted's mum says, leaving the room and rushing into the kitchen. My God, I feel sorry for her. I run after her and offer to help.

'No dear, honestly, you go back in there and have a good time….' But she looks sad and broken down by the pressure of dealing with Ted's dad.

I go back into the sitting room, where Ted and his father are in uncomfortable silence.

I have some presents for you,' I say, digging into my bag and pulling out the wrapped Christmas presents I had retrieved from under the bed earlier.

'Here you go,' I say, handing a gift to Ted's father.

Ted's mum has come into the room behind me, so I turn and hand her a carefully wrapped package as well.

'Thank you, dear,' she says, turning to her husband: 'Isn't that kind of Mary?'

'But what is it?' says Ted's dad. He opens his package to find a pretend aeroplane inside it. It's brightly painted and made of plastic. He throws it across the room, and we watch as it glides, dips, and flies.

'That's a lovely present,' says Ted's mum, though I detect the confusion in her voice.

I feel myself go scarlet. Why the hell have I got kids'

presents under my bed? I don't know any kids... Oh! I remember now; the presents were from when I played Father Christmas at a friend's party last year. They were the gifts I was giving out in the grotto, and there were too many of them, so I brought a few home. There is no chance on earth that the present that Ted's mum is about to open will be any more appropriate for her than the aeroplane was for Ted's dad.

'Goodness, that's nice. It might be a bit small, though,' she says, having opened the package to reveal a cowboy outfit.

Ted is just staring at me. 'Do you want to talk us through this?' he says as his mum makes a valiant attempt to wear a cowboy hat and pin the sheriff's badge onto her dress.

'I'm so sorry,' I say. 'I saw Ted had gifts for my mum and dad, and I wanted to bring something for you. I knew there were presents under my bed, so I went to get them. I've just remembered that they were presents for children. I'm such an idiot. I thought they were boxes of chocolates. I'm sorry.'

'No, not at all,' says Ted's mum. 'You know what they say; it's the thought that counts.'

'Don't worry,' says Ted, hugging me. 'Mum's going to look cracking in her new outfit.'

Ted's dad is just sitting in an almighty, slovenly heap. I'm starting to miss the relative warmth and happiness of my house.

'You know what we should do after lunch,' I say. 'We should invite my parents to join us...then we could play games and have a lovely time.'

'Oh dear, that would be marvellous,' says Ted's mum, positively beaming with excitement.

'Let me go and call them,' I say.

'Are you sure?' asks Ted. 'I mean - will they want to come?'

'I'll find out,' I say, and I head out of the room to make the silliest call ever. I have to confess to mum and dad that we are at Ted's for our second Christmas lunch of the day, and I have to ask them to come over in an hour and join us, but they mustn't mention the first lunch.

'Please, mum,' I say. 'I know it's a lot to ask, but it would make Christmas wonderful. I promise I'll explain all afterwards. Is that OK?'

'Of course, it is, dear,' says mum. 'I'll tell your dad.'

She takes the address and says they will be here in an hour.

I walk into the kitchen where Ted's mum is shaking a pan laden with roast potatoes. 'They are coming,' I tell her, and the look on her face says everything...she's delighted not to have to spend the day coping with her husband's miserable attitude and to have lots of other people to entertain.

'Let me tell everyone.'

She runs into the front room and announces that my parents are coming over.

'Oh great,' says Ted's dad, unenthusiastically.

'Oh,' says Ted. 'I see. Mary, can I have a word?'

Ted and I disappear into the back room, and I tell Ted how sad his mum looked and how much I'd like to cheer her up.

'If my parents come, we can play games, and it'll be noisy and fun and Christmassy. Your mum will love it.'

'You are lovely,' says Ted, hugging me. 'But won't they tell Mum that we were there earlier?'

'Mum's promised not to say anything,' I explain. 'Let's just make Christmas come alive for your mum.'

'Thank you,' says Ted. 'Now, can I ask you something?'

'Yes,' I say.

'Will you move in with me? Can we live together...you know - sometime soon? I mean - not immediately - but...in the future?'

'Oh my God, Ted, I'd love to. I'd love to.'

'That's sorted then,' he says. 'You and me - setting up home together. Happy Christmas, Mary Brown.'

'Happy Christmas, darling Ted,' I say.

Best. Christmas. Ever.

WANT TO KNOW WHAT HAPPENS NEXT?

Of course, you do!

See: Mary Brown is leaving Town. OUT NOW

UK: My Book

US: My Book

In the next book, Mary heads to Portugal for a weight loss camp and discovers it's nothing like she expected.

"I thought it would be Slimming World in the sunshine, but this is bloody torture," she says, after boxing, running, sand training (sand training? what fresh hell is sand training?), more running, more star jumps and eating nothing but carrots.

Mary wants to hide from the instructors and cheat the system. The trouble is, her mum is with her and won't leave her alone for a second... Then there's the angry instructor with a deep, dark secret about why he left the army. The mysterious woman who sneaks into their pool and does synchronised swimming every night. Who the hell is she? Why's she in their pool?

Mary obviously takes snacks in with her. Will they prevent her from losing any weight at all? And what about Yvonne - the slim, attractive lady who sneaks off every night after dinner? Where's she going? And what unearthly difficulties will Mary get herself into when she decides to follow her to find out...

While Mary's away on her retreat, she and Ted are forced to rethink their relationship. Ted doesn't have the time to see

Mary because he's working all the time, and Mary is getting very fed up with the situation. Reluctantly, our lovely couple decide to go their separate ways, leaving Mary alone.

She decides to try online dating sites.

Aided and abetted by her friends, including Juan Pedro – the flamboyant Spaniard whom she met when he was a dancer in sparkly trousers on a cruise ship, and best friend Charlie, Mary heads out on NINE DATES IN NINE DAYS.

She meets an interesting collection of men, including those she nicknames: Usain Bolt, Harry the Hoarder, and Dead-Wife-Darren.

Then just when she thinks things can't get any worse, Juan organises a huge, entirely inadvisable party at the end.

It's internet dating like you've never known it before…

"So INCREDIBLY FUNNY. **Read this book before you go on any internet dates.**"

"**I loved it. If you join an online dating site and go on dates, then make sure the guy doesn't have a big bag with him or a young kid. This really made me laugh.**"

'**I just loved it.**'

A wonderful book.'

"**It was hysterical, some bits made me laugh out loud, and other parts made me blush with recognition.**"

"**This is definitely one of my favourite of Mary's adventures so far! I feel like they're just getting better and better! Can't wait for the next one!!**"

UK
My Book
US

My Book
Thank you for your support xx

ALSO BY BERNICE BLOOM

There are lots more Mary Brown books in the series.
They can all be found on Amazon at:

UK

https://www.amazon.co.uk/Bernice-Bloom/e/B01MPZ5SBA?ref=
sr_ntt_srch_lnk_1&qid=1666995551&sr=8-1

US

https://www.amazon.com/Bernice-Bloom/e/B01MPZ5SBA?ref=
sr_ntt_srch_lnk_1&qid=1666995644&sr=1-1

**THE ORDER OF THE MARY BROWN BOOKS (Ebook readers
can click 'My Book' for more details):**

1. WHAT'S UP, MARY BROWN?: My Book

2. THE ADVENTURES OF MARY BROWN: My Book

3. CHRISTMAS WITH MARY BROWN: My Book

4. MARY BROWN IS LEAVING TOWN: My Book

5. MARY BROWN IN LOCKDOWN: My Book

6. MYSTERIOUS INVITATION: My Book

7. CONFESSIONS

8. MARY BROWN GETS A PUPPY

9. DON'T MENTION THE HEN WEEKEND: My Book

10. THE ST LUCIA MYSTERY (out end 2023)

THE ORDER OF THE SUNSHINE COTTAGE BOOKS:

1 RETURN TO SUNSHINE COTTAGE (OUT NOW): My Book

2 GIRLS AT SUNSHINE COTTAGE (PRE-ORDER) My Book

3 VALENTINE'S DAY AT SUNSHINE COTTAGE (10/02/2023): My Book

4 LIFE AT SUNSHINE COTTAGE (03/07/2023) My Book

5 CHRISTMAS AT SUNSHINE COTTAGE (01/12/2023): My Book

6 SUMMER AT SUNSHINE COTTAGE (01/06/2024)

Printed in Great Britain
by Amazon

27149190R00111